RABBIT EARS

RABBIT EARS

MAGGIE DE VRIES

HarperTrophyCanada

Rabbit Ears
Copyright © 2014 by Maggie de Vries.
All rights reserved.

Published by Harper*Trophy*Canada™, an imprint
of HarperCollins Publishers Ltd.

First edition

HarperCollins books may be purchased for educational, business, or sales
promotional use through our Special Markets Department.

HarperCollins Publishers Ltd
2 Bloor Street East, 20th Floor
Toronto, Ontario, Canada
M4W 1A8

www.harpercollins.ca

Library and Archives Canada Cataloguing in Publication
information is available upon request.

ISBN 978-1-44341-662-7

Printed and bound in Canada
WEB 9 8 7 6 5 4 3 2 1

To sisters and friends.
In memory of my sister Sarah and my friend Amanda.

CHAPTER ONE

Kaya

Cities don't get dark. You thought they did, but they don't. Not dark like this.

The blackness excites you, zipping sparks through your arms and legs. And you look up. Up. Up past the trees to the stars. Thousands. Millions. Billions of them. The sparks shoot right into your skull, zap your eye sockets; you suck in air and feel your face open into a massive grin.

Once you are on the dirt driveway out of sight of the old summer-house, you turn on your light, but it's still tough picking your way down the slope to the road. It's pitch-dark here too, on the pavement. No street lights. You're more likely to be run down than picked up. Still, the grin won't leave you. The sparks go on zipping away inside.

Your penlight doesn't give you much to go by, but you stride along anyway, trusting the pavement to meet your feet, twirling once in a while, stirring up a breeze, breathing in the smell of the trees, the ocean salt and the dark. After a while you hear a car, turn and shine the light on yourself, standing well away from the road. The car flies by. You thrust your fist into the air, shine your little light on it and raise your middle finger, hoping the asshole's looking in his rear-view mirror. And on you stride. You'll walk all the way if you have to.

Another car. This one slows down beside you, and stops.

You walk over and lean in the open window. The driver flips on the inside light, and your grin drops from your face. A white-haired man is alone in the car, hunched over the steering wheel, like it's attached to him or something. A comb-over flops across his forehead. For a second you think . . . but no. Still, you step back. Your blood has stopped burning. Your body has stopped vibrating. You do not want a ride from this man. He leans just a little in your direction, a kind of furrowed smile on his face.

"Where are you off to, young lady?" he says.

You tell the truth. "Big Tribune."

"All on your own?"

"I'm meeting friends." Forget the truth. "They . . . they'll be along any minute."

He squints as he peers up at you, but you turn the flashlight off so that he is looking from light into dark.

"All right, then," he says at last. "I hope you'll be careful."

"I always am," you say, letting him see your best copy of a smile.

As he pulls away, you breathe relief.

You walk on. You're not going back to that house. You won't. Your blood stays cool, though. You shiver, even with the sweater. Your flip-flops wear away at your toes.

Beth

Despite the sputtering fan, it's hot in the room at the top of the ramshackle house, but I don't care. Sweat trickles down the back of my neck; my T-shirt sticks to my back, but it doesn't matter. I love it here. Later, when my light is out and all the bats are asleep in the rafters, I'll open the floor-to-ceiling window and fall asleep in the late-August midnight breeze. For now, my light is on. I am arranging my beach glass on the windowsill.

I turn the newest piece over and over. I love its dull smoothness, all its shine and sharp edges worn away by the sea. This one is pale pink; its ridges once formed part of a letter. An *a* maybe. I settle it into its spot and crab-crawl back across my mattress to sit with my back flat to the wall. *Sabriel* lies spine up, pages splayed, on the bed beside me, but I don't feel like reading.

I look at my watch. 10:14. Mom is probably asleep. And Kaya too, I guess. I was worried about Kaya and the island nights. Petrified, actually. I know what goes on here, the raves and things, and she's just barely thirteen. The first few nights, I stayed up late, and even after I went to bed, I slipped back down, over and over, and peeked into her room. She was always snug in bed by ten. You'd never know she's the kind of kid to get in so much trouble.

Kaya

You are out of the trees when the next car comes by, and the moon is lighting up the horizon, just getting ready to rise. The car pulls to a stop, laughter pouring from its open windows. It's full of girls. Jammed.

"You off to Big Trib?" one shouts at you, much too loud with the car pulled up close.

"Course she is," another voice shouts as the back door swings open. "Hop in."

And you do, fitting yourself into a sliver of space after the girl who opened the door shifts onto a nearby lap.

At first the talk and laughter flow over you. You give short answers to one or two questions, but in your head you're still out there on the road, shivering and sore.

"You're a bit of a downer," one of them says. "Here, have a swig of this."

She's reaching around from the front seat, holding out a mickey. Just the sight of it warms you up, starting in your gut.

You take a swig and sputter. "What the hell *is* this?"

"Bit of this, bit of that," the girl next to you says.

"Well, it's disgusting," you say as it snugs into a cozy, warm ball in your chest. You take another gulp.

"Hey, leave some for the rest of us!" the lap-rider shouts, and you pass it along, but the gross concoction has done its job. The sparks are back.

They have to park a long way from the beach, and they have a lot of stuff to carry. "Thanks for the ride," you say as they unpack the car. "I'm just going to—"

"What? You're going to take off on us? Come on! At least you can carry one end of the cooler."

"You might not like the beach on your own," hop-in girl says.

"Oh, I'll be all right," you say. "I'm meeting some people. Thanks again." You take several steps backward into the dark.

"Let her go," another girl says. "Some people are just ungrateful."

"Hey, I said thanks," you say, but by then the dark has swallowed you. You turn and walk a long way down the road before you flip on your light.

It takes a while to find the short bit of trail that leads out onto the sand, and you listen for those girls catching up. There's something about girls all together like that. You'll take a bunch of guys any day. At last an entwined couple stumbles onto the road right in front of you. They can only have come along the trail. You've found it. Light aimed at the ground, you pick your way through the narrow band of trees. Sound reaches you first: a rumble of voices punctuated by roars and shouts; the crackling of the nearest fires; the swooshing of waves washing high on the beach. You come out of the trees and stop.

The beach is nothing like it was in the afternoon. The tide has consumed it, all but the heaps of driftwood that line the beach above the tide-line. The wood makes ghostly shapes in the dark, and moonlight makes a white stripe across the expanse of water, ending right at your feet. Along the water's edge to your left and all the way down to the dark cliffs at the other end of the beach: orange-red flames and the dark shadows of partiers.

Excitement licks at you as you remember Adam from the afternoon, the tilt of his grin, the tattooed ring around his upper arm, the sand dried into his hair.

A fire would be great. Your thin sweater is not keeping

out the midnight chill. But the water calls to you too. The water and the moon.

After all, tomorrow morning you are leaving the island, heading home, back to dry land, dry life.

Δ

You thought today's afternoon swim was your last. This afternoon you dove deep, but your life followed you. Your life reached down, down, down into the water of the bay, grasped you in one grimy paw, squeezed your mouth open with the other, and shoved itself right down your throat.

Furious, you surfaced and gasped for air, stood in the shallows staring at a round red umbrella. You couldn't see her from that distance, but you knew your mother was there. She had brought you to this island to keep you safe, but tomorrow she was taking you home. Not just home . . . to school. High school.

You stumbled onto the shore, heading away from the families to the part of the beach where the leftover hippies hang out.

It's 1997; flower power is long gone, but some of these people haven't heard.

Δ

Now, in the moonlit night, you are in need of one last Hornby Island swim. Adam will just have to wait.

Instead of turning left toward the beach, you turn right, away from the line of fires, and pick your way along the shore toward the point. No sand here, just rock, and water has overrun almost all of it, so you are alone. The moon lights your way, and, after a bit, you reach a jutting rock almost in the shadow of the trees. You sit. The moon has followed you and you look up at it, wondering. It is a little more than half of itself, a sort of oblong lump. But still. The moon's the moon.

The water makes peaceful lapping sounds right near your toes. The fires and the partiers seem far away. The humid air feels warm, suddenly; you stop shivering and gaze at the calm water, at the boats that float mirage-like near where you swam in the afternoon.

You push off your flip-flops first. Then you stand and let the damp cool of the stone sink into your soles, smooth and delicious. Just in case the tide isn't done rising, you put your shoes side by side, up high where you have been sitting. You take off your sweater, ball it up and tuck your bag in the middle. That goes on top of the shoes. Your dress comes next.

For a moment you stand naked in the moonlight.

Then you walk into the water, feet certain on the stone.

The water has barely reached your thighs when you crouch, lean forward and tip yourself in. In the water you change. You become a creature of the sea. Your skin is as slick as a seal's pelt; your feet, as flexible as flippers; your legs and torso, designed for the deeps.

The water is very cold, but that hardly bothers you at all. Eyes wide, you swim every which way, following the sparkling light as it tries to reach the bottom of the sea. Then, still deep down, you flip onto your back, look up and see the moon itself.

You're under water on earth, you think, and you're look-ing at the moon. It occurs to you to fill yourself up with water, to draw it deep into your lungs, weigh yourself down with it, so that your body sinks and you lie forever on the ocean floor gazing up at the moon, at the stars, at the sun, through unblinking eyes, as time passes on and on in the dry-land world, as nights turn to days and to nights again. You would never have to be that girl again.

You part your lips and feel the water on your tongue. Releasing a string of bubbles as you go, you shoot to the sur-face for some air. The cold is getting the better of you. You need one of those roaring fires right about now.

Moments later, standing full out of the water with the moonlight at your back, you see two figures sitting right where your clothes are supposed to be.

"I told you she'd be naked," one of them says.

Beth

The heat wakes me up, and I roll over on the hard bed and toss the sheet off. It's all tangled up with my ankles and I sit up to get it free. Sweat dribbles—actually dribbles—out of my hair and down my neck. I swipe at it and stare out into the black. The air in the room is heavy and still. Bats will be tucked up in the rafters by now, and I decide to take my chan-ces with the mosquitoes. Time to let the outside in.

Without switching on the light, I feel my way to the win-dow latch, careful not to mess with my bits of glass. Window open, I let that cool air wash over me, take a deep breath, heave myself to my feet and head for the door. I need to pee.

On the landing, one floor down, I stop. The door to Kaya's room is ajar. A familiar fear ripples through my rib cage and into my belly. She must have left the door open to let in some air. Seconds tick by as I listen for the sound of some nice deep-sleep breathing. The silence hurts my head. I could just carry on to the bathroom and go back to bed.

No, I could not. I push. The door opens and I slip through. Once in, I know the bed is empty, but I check anyway. Sybilla whines softly and I reach down and stroke her. The dog is curled up right on Kaya's pillow, even though she's too big for it, and Kaya is gone.

I think for the briefest moment about waking Mom, about getting in the car, searching the island, tracking down my wayward sister.

But letting Mom know seems so awful, so real. And Mom's jittery weeping—I can't take another minute of that. How likely is it that we'd find Kaya anyway?

I go down to the bathroom, pee, come back up and slip into Kaya's bed, pushing Sybilla down onto the rug.

I'm going to wait for her right here.

Kaya

Your seal's pelt, your flippers, the wonders of the deep— they all drop away. You stand wet and cold in your human skin; a shiver runs the length of your body and brings your teeth clanking together. Feeling a spurt of rage, you step forward. No one is going to humiliate you.

"Get away from my clothes," you say, and take another step.

You can make out the two boys in the moonlight. Drunk and stupid.

"I said, step away from my clothes."

"Hey, we'll give you your clothes when we feel like it," one says, but the other has already sidled off a bit.

They don't try to stop you when you walk right up, snatch your dress and put it on. "What are you? Twelve?" you say as you force your wet arms into the sleeves of your sweater. Your bag falls and you have to scramble for it.

"Fourteen," the sidler says.

"Shut up, Justin." That's the other one.

You will your heart to slow down and your body to warm up. You really need one of those fires. And you do not like the clenched teeth in the boy's voice when he tells his friend to shut up.

"I'm cold," you say. "I'm going to find a fire." Then, "Come if you want." That way, if they choose to follow, it's at your invitation. You hope you'll find the guys who smoked you up before the two dweebs find their friends. You don't want to deal with a whole pack of boys.

You walk in the shallows, peering into the gatherings around the fires, searching for anyone familiar. The beach is alive with bodies, with shouts, with laughter and fire, and the heavy smell of smoke. Excitement prickles at you, but you stay well back, for now.

The girls from the car are the first people you recognize, and you pick up your pace, hoping that Justin and his friend will drop off. These girls seem more their speed. The boys probably haven't seen many naked girls in their lives, though—maybe you are the first—because they stick to you like pollen on a bee.

"Where are you going?" Justin asks more than once.

"You don't have to come," you reply.

You wrung out your annoying quantities of hair before you put on your sweater, but it still sends a river down your back. Your dress clings to your skin. The beach goes on forever. This afternoon the guys with the tokes were at the far end. That's where they should be now, but it's hard to tell who's who in the dark. You don't want to walk up and peer right into faces.

"Hey, babe," a voice shouts from one of the fires, "come have a beer."

"No, thanks," you call back, and walk on.

As you approach another fire, a figure turns, looks for a moment and stumbles toward the water. "Hey, babe," he says as he falls into lumbering step beside you.

What is it with these guys? Is that the only phrase they know? Fear thickens your limbs, dulls the prickles.

The guy stops dead, half blocking your path. "You're wet," he slurs.

"Yeah," you say. "And I'm with him." You grab Justin's arm and pull him to your side. He looks at you in surprise.

As soon as you've put those guys behind you, you drop Justin's arm and pick up your pace.

"We're, uh . . . we're going to head back," he says when the cliffs at the north end of the beach loom close. The other guy, the gruff one, does not meet your eyes before they turn.

Well, at least you're rid of them.

Feet back on dry sand, you look up the beach toward the last in the long line of fires. It lights a wooden shelter, massive and intricate—a shelter you recognize. You sat there this afternoon, talking to a bunch of hippies while your bikini dried. The sight of the familiar driftwood construction lit by an enormous blaze sends that wild, free feeling through you again, much stronger now. Your whole body tingles.

You walk closer. "Adam?" you call.

A man steps away from the group, backlit by the fire, frontlit by the moon.

"You're wet," he says.

"I went for a swim."

"Hey, guys," he calls over his shoulder, "uh . . ."

"Kaya," you say.

"Kaya is back."

Another guy jumps up and offers you a spot on a log near the fire. Adam puts a beer into your hand and a girl with dreadlocks passes you a fat joint. You take a swig and a toke and hold out your legs toward the flames. Energy courses around the fire, bottles clank and a log collapses, sending a whoosh of flames and sparks into the dark. You breathe the smell of woodsmoke and soak in the warmth. Your face and your shoulders relax.

Adam sits down beside you and puts his hand on your knee. He lives on the big island and comes over here as much as he can in the summer. He doesn't really work or go to school; he was a bit vague this afternoon on what he actually does, but so were you. He's tall and slim but not skinny. His skin is so smooth and kind of gleaming that in the heat of the afternoon, you wanted to run your finger down the centre of his bare chest. He's clean-shaven and his thick, dark hair is pulled back into a stubby ponytail.

"You came a long way to find us tonight," he says, "all by yourself."

You let your shoulder rise and fall against his. "I was bored at home," you say.

Beth

A gasp wakes me, followed by a single word—"Beth?"—and a soft bark shushed.

I sit up, confused, and stare into the black. I smell wood-smoke.

"What are you doing in my bed?" Kaya says.

"What were you doing *out* of it?" I hiss. I'm in Kaya's bed, that's where I am.

"It's none of your business," Kaya says. "Get out of here."

Not so fast, I think, as I reach out and flip on the lamp. It takes her only a second to flip it off again, but a second is long enough. Her hair hangs in heavy damp clumps around her face and a big black sooty smear runs up one side of her dress. Her legs and arms are covered in long red scratches. She doesn't look like someone who was just partying with other kids. Sybilla is weaving back and forth against those marked-up legs, whining with delight.

"You're hurt," I say, reaching again for the switch.

Kaya blinks hard at the bright light, closes her eyes and leans against the wall.

"I'm not hurt, Beth. I just need to sleep," she says.

"Please, can you leave me alone?" Then she surprises me. She straightens and stands by the bed, does a little twirl, tops it with a curtsy. "See? It's all good. Now. Go. Back. To. Bed."

And I do. I climb the stairs, collapse on my bed and pull the thin sheet over my head to keep the mosquitoes at bay. I fall asleep quickly in the gentle breeze, relieved that my sister, whatever she may have got into tonight, is tucked away now in her own bed.

Kaya

"How old did you say you were?" Adam asks after a while.

You tilt your head and grin. "Sixteen." You don't need to ask him his age. He told you back in the afternoon. He's nineteen. All grown up.

"And where are you from?"

"Vancouver," you say, puzzled. He ought to remember that.

"No, I mean where are you really from?"

It takes you a minute to understand what he means. Then you see him looking at your brown skin and you get it. Annoying, but you decide to let it go.

"I was actually born right in Vancouver," you say. "I was adopted. My family is white."

"Oh," he says. He wraps his arm around your shoulder, pulls you close and kisses your forehead. Your body nestles itself against him and he responds, lowering his lips to yours.

"You want to go for a walk?" he says in your ear.

He pulls you to your feet. The two of you start off down the beach.

Dreadlock girl calls after him. "Hey. Where you going?"

"Just a walk," Adam shouts back.

The tide has receded a bit, and you walk at the water's edge, stopping now and then to kiss in the moonlight. As if from a distance, you watch yourself standing ankle-deep in the ocean, with a gorgeous guy's arm hooked around you, his lips soft as whispers, his tongue sleek in your mouth.

This is how it's supposed to be, you think. This is perfect. You walk with your hand on his bare waist, feeling his muscles flex as he walks, feeling how strong he is.

You are so caught up in your vision that you hardly notice that you're leaving the beach, walking through the band of trees, coming out on the road. Before you take in that that's where he's leading you, he's unlocking his car.

You don't even hesitate. You get in, but you watch yourself doing it, nervous anticipation thick in your limbs.

When he gathers you into his arms, your stomach flips right over and electricity shoots straight into your crotch. You tense and squirm away a bit. He sits back and grasps your shoulders.

"Let's go to my place," he says, his voice the tenderest thing.

"I . . . I can't," you say. "I have to get home."

Abruptly, he lets go of you and starts the car, pulls out. "Which way?" he says when he reaches the main road. He follows your instructions and makes the left turn. He doesn't go far, though, before he turns down a dirt road, pulls over and turns off the car.

"No need to go home this instant," he says, and kisses you again, with a lot more tongue than before. His hand grasps your breast for a moment, through your dress, and drops to your thigh. It feels heavy now, tentacled, and it starts to crawl up your skirt.

All the electricity is gone. Your body is on lockdown.

You manage a muffled but insistent "no" around his tongue. His hand retreats.

Relief, of a sort, washes through you—until you hear his zipper. Your right arm drifts for the door handle. He pulls his face away from yours and looks down, and you follow his gaze to his crotch. At the sight of his erect penis, you snap your lids shut.

"Come on," he says, his voice thick. "You don't want to leave me like this, do you?"

You open your eyes, and he reaches out, works his fingers into your hair and pulls at your head. You push back against his hand and turn your face toward that door.

"Tease," he says.

That's it. That's all he has to say. You let him pull your head down and you do what he wants.

You watch yourself performing the act, and something clicks into place inside you. The romance in the shallows, the moonlit kisses, none of that is you. It never has been.

Anyway, "the act" doesn't take long at all. He lets go of your head right away and you rear up and stare straight ahead, filled with a kind of tarry darkness, a miserable calm.

"I'll drive you home now," he says then, and you turn to look at him. The moonlight is still streaming into the car, flooding him now with cold white light. He reaches for the keys. You wipe your face with your sleeve. Loathing leaks into that big calm space inside you.

"No," you say. "I'll walk."

You thrust the door open and tumble straight into the ditch, which is full of brambles. Up the other side you go, scrapes and scratches burning, trying to keep your breathing quiet, trying to muster a shred of pride.

He gets out of the car and walks along the ditch. "Hey," he calls. "Come on. I'm just going to drive you home."

"I said I'll walk," you call back.

"What's the matter with you?" he shouts. Then, a long silence.

At last he gets back in his car and drives along slowly. Eventually, he's off the gravel, onto the pavement, and gone. You wait a bit longer in the silent night; then you creep back onto the road and start the long walk home.

Other girls don't do that, you're guessing. They don't take rides with strangers who want to have sex with them. They don't exchange oral sex for taxi service. Well, you didn't do that either, you think, as you put one sore foot in front of the other.

As you walk, ignoring blisters and scratches, you think back briefly to the moon shining through the water, reaching its light into the depths to touch you. You don't deserve that clean beauty, you think.

And with the thought comes a sort of black satisfaction. You are, you really are, *that* girl.

Mom is turning the fridge inside out, no sign of breakfast, when I come down at eight thirty with my arms full of sheets. She has a big mug of coffee on the go, almost certainly cold. And she's in a state.

So much to do. Ferry leaves in two hours.

We won't be catching that one, I think. Mom always sets her sights on the impossible and then is furious when the impossible is just that.

"I'm capable of helping, Mom," I say as I head for the washing machine in the pantry. It's already running, so I dump my armload on the floor and head back to the kitchen. "I'm always helping." I know I sound whiny, but I can't help it. "Do you think I could have some breakfast first?"

Mom gestures broadly. "Help yourself," she says.

And I look around at the chaos. Ah, granola. And there's the milk on the counter.

First few bites consumed. "Kaya's the one who really should be helping," I say, tempted, oh so tempted, to tell Mom about my early morning vigil. It was two o'clock when I crept back into bed. Two!

"Shall I go wake her?" I ask, but Mom doesn't even glance in my direction.

"Kaya's not much good in the morning," she says, as if I don't already know that.

I finish my breakfast and go upstairs to pack my own room, feet banging on the stairs. I shove Kaya's door open as I pass. A grunt from her tangled bed rewards me. What did happen to her out there? How did she get those scratches?

I don't care, I tell myself. But not caring is hard work.

I'm quick with my own stuff, and with the broom and dustpan on the wide wooden planks. Bag and broom thump down the stairs behind me. Back to Kaya's door.

She sits up as I walk in. Sybilla is up on the bed with her, her huge collie bulk nestled against Kaya's legs. Kaya isn't supposed to let her up there, but she does, every night, and Mom knows it. How did it happen that that dog became all Kaya's anyway?

"Leave me alone," Kaya says. "I'm up."

"What happened to you last night?" I say. It's a direct question, and my mouth stays open, lips pulled back on the *t*, surprised at itself.

Her eyes meet mine for an instant. "Nothing happened. I went out. I came back. And found you where you shouldn't have been."

I look at her, hair knotted, skin grey instead of brown, eyes squinting. Unlike me, Kaya is a beauty, but you'd never know it to look at her now.

"I was worried," I say. Or whisper.

That beaten-down face fixes itself into a sneer. "What?" she says.

I back down, as usual. "Nothing," I say. "Just get ready. Mom wants to catch the noon boat off the island."

Kaya glances at her wrist and shrugs. "Mom always wants things she can't get," she says.

I leave then, anger and shame battling each other deep in my belly, and turn my attention to sweeping and scrubbing the bathroom, which is spotless by the time I'm done.

CHAPTER TWO

Beth

Back home. September. Kaya's first day of high school. I keep an eye out. Who's she going to talk to? Where's she going to go between classes?

I see her at the start of lunch, her head up and back, that little self-satisfied sneer plastered all over her face, strutting—like, actually strutting—her way out to the breezeway. Ten minutes later, I catch a glimpse of her through a window and she's all by herself, kind of shrunken up against the wall.

I want to go out there and yell at the other kids, order them to be nice to my sister. Or yell at her, *Smile! Knock that rock off your shoulder. You look like a stuck-up little* . . . My mind draws back from that word and all words like it. I wander off and leave her on her own.

I can't believe that my thirteen-year-old sister actually got caught shoplifting. And not something small like a chocolate bar or a sparkly barrette, but jeans. She got caught stealing a pair of jeans. And not when she was out with a pack of girls.

Or on her own, even. She was shopping with Mom. She got caught shoplifting when she was out with *her mother*.

Sometimes I wonder if we know everything that went on with Kaya last year. Grade Seven. The jeans incident was the first bad thing we knew about, but what if there's more? Sometimes I get this sick feeling, like when Kaya came back all scratched up. I'm pretty sure that we don't know the half of it.

The trip to Hornby was meant to be the big cure, but I'm kind of afraid that it didn't do a thing to help. Not one thing. It's like Kaya is on a quick tumble—down, down, down—not on the *road* to hell, more like one of those "death drop" slides they have at water parks.

The other kids aren't all that nice to me either. It's not like I'm one of the ones who gets listened to. Except for Jane and Samantha, that is, or "the bully and the waif," as I call them in my imaginings. My friends.

I get my lunch out of my locker and finger the change in my pocket, searching for paper. There should be a five-dollar bill left over from Saturday. Jane and Samantha will be waiting at the end of the next hall, in our lunch spot. It's the first day of school, and we've barely had a chance to talk to each other all morning. Jane will want to know all about how it went on Hornby with the delinquent. Samantha will be sweetly soothing. My fingers find the bill, clutch it, and I head for the nearest door.

My jeans are pinching at my waist. I know that rolls show through my shirt, even though I picked my loosest one this morning. But I can feel my teeth sinking through chewy candy—Fuzzy Peach, I'm thinking—the burst of sweet and sour together and the soothing lumps of gelatin sliding down my throat. I don't need my weird friends and their fake sympathy right now. I need the real thing, and it comes in a package from the corner store just down the street.

Kaya

You're standing there outside, all hunched over, when you see Michelle for the first time. She's coming round the corner into the open, pulling a cigarette out of her pocket, even though you're not allowed to smoke out here. Her hair is long, black and as bone-straight as yours is curly. Her body is kind of thick, her shoulders curved forward, but in an "I'm ready to mow you down" kind of a way.

She's standing there, alone, not looking at anyone, when the girls come up to you in a little cluster. Three of them. Probably Grade Nine, but you really have no idea.

"What's your name?" one of them, tall, pale, big teeth, says.

"Kaya."

"Hey, Kaya." Slightly too much emphasis on the first syllable. "You're new, aren't you?"

You nod, just barely, nervous now.

"Let's go for a walk. We'll show you around."

No one ever approached you at school all the way through Grade Seven, and here in Grade Eight it's happening on your first day. Maybe kids are friendlier here. You look at the other two girls. Neither is especially pretty. One is tallish, thin and white, in a skirt and knee socks; the other is average height, thicker, Asian maybe, in jeans. All three look like they got new outfits for back-to-school.

"Come on," the toothy girl says. "It's so pretty!"

Toothy girl leads the four of you around the corner of the building you were leaning against, away from the entrance. And there are the woods; a reddish brown trail meanders off into the shadows. It *is* pretty. A girl on either side of you, you walk into the trees.

Then, "Ugly bitch." The words are hissed and come with a shove. You hit the ground hard, and scrabble off the path instinctively, even before your mind catches up with what is happening.

They stand over you, poking at you with their feet, blocking any escape, pelting you with words. "You were standing in our spot, back there," the jeaned girl says. "We don't let dirty Blacks like you in our space."

You shrink into a ball, arms around your head. Your inside self just curls up on the ground, gives in instantly. Shame curdles your blood.

And then the whole group flies apart. The words *whirling dervish* spring into your mind as you raise your head to see the cement-faced, cigarette-wielding girl crashing right into the bunch of you, shouting, "Leave her alone!"

There's something about her attitude, something about her fury, that stops those girls instantly. They wander off grumbling, with only a few angry glances and weak parting shots.

She stands over you for a moment before she holds out a hand to help you up. "I'm Michelle," she says, leaning against a tree and taking a drag of her cigarette, which has survived her attack on the girls.

And that's how you and Michelle get to be friends, sort of. She's mostly silent, a loner, but she tolerates your company, you tolerate hers, and as long as the two of you are together, those girls don't bother either of you, and neither does anybody else. You attend classes sometimes. Sometimes you don't. Michelle is away sometimes. And sometimes she's there.

Δ

One Monday at the end of September.

"What would you like for breakfast, honey?" Mom says. "Quick, quick, else you'll be late for school."

She hasn't crashed yet, just home from twelve straight hours at the hospital. There's food in the house and the dishes are washed for a change. It's been kind of depressing at home since Hornby. Mom hates night shift.

"You know I don't eat breakfast," you say. "And I'm always on time for school."

Beth looks up from her massive bowl of granola—everyone knows you're only supposed to eat a little bit of that stuff. "Liar," she says.

Your gut clenches. If you eat, you'll throw up on the spot.

"I'm not a liar," you scream at them both. "I am not!" And you're running for the door, and Mom is running after you.

This doesn't make any sense, you think as you run. Not to them. Not even to you. And you keep right on running.

Mom follows you all the way out onto the sidewalk, so

you turn and scream again. "Can't you see I'm going? I'm going to school like you want me to. Leave me alone!" You're screaming so loud it might make your throat bleed. You wish it would. You'd love to spit great gobs of blood onto the pavement right about now.

Mom turns and heads back into the house. Her slumped shoulders send a river of pain through you, but you grit your teeth and flush it away. You're going to school. That's what she wanted. Right?

Please, please, please let Michelle be there today.

And she is. You find her out in the breezeway, just minutes to go before the first bell. The two of you head into the woods.

"Can I bum a cigarette?" you say. The first cigarette of your life.

She looks at you, slight puzzlement wrinkling that cement brow of hers. "What's up?" she says.

"My family's shit," you say.

The wrinkles smooth. Almost. And she hands you a cigarette, lights it for you.

You pull the smoke into your body, fill yourself up with it, hack, cough, blow out, and marvel at the smooth cloud of smoke that flows from your lungs. Wow!

Michelle smiles a small smile.

"Let's take off for the day," you say, hoping your voice sounds eager instead of desperate. "Right now. Let's go downtown!"

That first afternoon, you take the bus to Granville, which is hopping. Half a dozen kids are strung out along the wall of a movie theatre, cap set out on top of a cardboard sign, collecting coins while they talk among themselves, pretty much ignoring the passersby. One has a collared cat on her shoulder, a bit of string standing in for a leash, but it's the dog that draws you in.

He's a mutt, scruffy, with a long nose and ears that neither stand up nor flop over. His tail is skinny and wags like anything when you hunker down beside him. With your fingers buried in his fur, it's easy to let Michelle introduce you, to smile, and slowly, slowly, to enter into the chatter.

You are home in time for supper (such as it is).

Δ

Another time, you say you are staying over at Michelle's and the two of you go downtown together at night. You sneak into her basement room late, late, still fizzing with excitement, giggling when you trip over something in the dark.

Then Michelle goes off on her own one day and doesn't come back for a week. Her parents call, but you don't tell them anything. You have nothing to tell. You look for her yourself along Granville, but no one's seen her in days.

At last she shows up at school one afternoon, but she's gone kind of glassy and weird.

"Where were you?" you say. "I went looking."

Her eyes skim past yours. "Nowhere," she says. And the next day she's gone again. This time you don't go looking. You have no idea where to look.

Δ

Eventually you go downtown on your own, just to be there, not to look for Michelle.

You can't find the kids. It's probably too early. So you wander along Granville, feeling your "real" life on the other side of town loosen its grip bit by bit, finger by finger, till it can be whisked away by the breeze, burnt off by the sunshine, cancelled out by all the strangers' lives, each dark untold story.

Farther down the street, people are setting up their stalls, jewellery mostly, and along the walls of the big white department store, Eaton's, the ones who don't have stalls are laying out their stuff on blankets on the ground. Only one is all set up already, and there you stop. You stand and watch for a bit without drawing attention to yourself. The woman is thin, hair braided back and wound round with stones. Her jeans are worn, her sandals ancient, her collarbone jagged. She's wearing one three-stoned pendant and several chunky rings.

You turn your attention from her to her work. She uses a sheet of burlap wrapped around a board and laid on the ground as backing. Pinned to it are dozens of earrings, bracelets and necklaces, all made with heavy string and semi-precious stones.

Beth would love this, you think, but the truth is, you love it yourself.

A year ago, you would have been planning how to get a pair of earrings into your pocket without her noticing, but the jeans incident seems to have cured you of shoplifting. Besides, you have a philosophy: stealing from corporations is one thing; stealing from battered-up people on the street is another.

You wander back down Granville, hoping that the kid with the scruffy mutt will be there. Or maybe Michelle. You've been trying not to think about her, but it's hard. You don't find the kid, or the mutt, or Michelle, but you end up toking up in a back alley with the girl with the cat. After that, you head home.

On the bus, you pull a crumpled wad of paper and a stubby pencil from your purse, sketch the girl with the cat on her shoulder and put down a few words about what that cat might see from up there. You look around at one point and see a man smiling at you from across the way. Whatever expression you had on your face while you were writing drops away. You toss the man your best scowl and shove paper and pencil out of sight.

Δ

It's November, wet and cold, and dark by five o'clock. And the "buy, buy, buy" of Christmas is taking over the city streets with its bundled-up throngs and a lot of damp sparkle.

The cold can't stop you. You go back twice more, skipping school, looking for Michelle. When you do go to school, you can hardly stand it for a minute. At home, you bite Mom's and Beth's heads off, crunch their bones between your teeth.

Michelle stays away.

Δ

Then, one day in early December, you are standing at your locker after lunch gearing up for math, when someone taps you on the shoulder. You jump, turn and freeze.

It's Diana.

Diana *at school*.

You're not sure what you do on the outside, but inside everything contracts. To give Diana credit, she looks scared. Petrified. Like a rabbit confronted with a weasel. But she is here. At your school. Looking you in the eye. And she has *touched* you.

"I just switched schools," she says, as if she thinks you might want to exchange words, you might want an explanation.

And how could she do that? How could she walk right into your school and make herself at home here? You stand, almost teetering. She is the weasel, not you. She is the weasel.

Except instead of sinking her teeth into your throat, she sucks memories up out of the mire.

You want to slap her or vomit. You feel your face contort and watch her recoil. How can she possibly expect anything else? What does she want? The questions tumble about in your head, but the answers don't matter. Escape does.

You click your locker shut, grit your teeth and push past her. "I've got class," you say. As you walk away, you shove the memories back down until the sludge slops over them, and they're gone. For now.

As you pass, you hear her draw breath to reply, but you get straight onto the next bus downtown. In your mind, that's the first time that counts as running away.

Δ

You're furious when they find you. Track you down like a common criminal.

You're just hanging out on the street with the cat girl and a bunch of other kids.

And sure, you might be passing around a bit of pot. But nothing else. Nothing else at all.

Then, right in front of you, there's Mom. "Kaya?" she says, as if you can't possibly be her precious daughter.

You look up, your lips come together on the *M* in "Mom," but you stop yourself. You get up and walk away from her. She's on your heels, so you break into a run. Five minutes later, a police officer's got you by the arm. An hour later, you're home.

Beth

I'm glad to see her. Of course I am. But I'm mad too. Furious, to be honest.

When the front door opens at midnight, I'm asleep on the couch. Mom's a nurse and supposed to be working night shift this week, but she called in sick when Kaya wasn't home by ten. By now, we're used to waiting for Kaya to come home. We know she's skipping school a fair bit. But she usually calls and tells us some story or other. Mom gobbles those lies up like bonbons. The difference today was no phone call. No nice little story.

So, like I said, Mom called in sick and set off in search. I was supposed to call her if Kaya called or turned up. Mom was supposed to call me if she found her. Well, I went to sleep and Mom didn't bother to call, so neither of us honoured our agreement exactly.

Before I fell asleep, I thought about calling Samantha, just to talk, imagined her kind voice on the phone, but she's not a secret-keeper, and I couldn't face talking about all this with Jane at school tomorrow, so I didn't.

Kaya comes in first, her face chalky with makeup, mascara smeared everywhere, tear tracks from eyes to chin. Mom's right behind her. Kaya doesn't even look in my direction. She yanks open the door to the stairs, lets Sybilla barrel past her, and turns on Mom.

"I was just minding my own business, and you set the police on me. The police! Do you know how humiliating that is? It wasn't even midnight yet. Why can't you just leave me alone?" she screeches, already halfway up the stairs.

"You're just a kid," Mom says after her. "You're my daughter." She's crying too, but at least she has no makeup to smudge. "And I love you."

But Kaya's bedroom door has already slammed, shaking the whole house, and she doesn't hear those last words.

Kaya

After the police turn you over to Mom, it gets still harder to stick around. And with Diana there, school feels impossible. You do try, though, even if Mom and Beth can't see it. You do. After the holidays, Michelle starts showing up sometimes, but she's cagey about where she's been. It's infuriating after the time you spent together downtown. Anyway, she doesn't look good. You stay away from her too.

In January, you start a metalwork class. It's actually kind

of fun for a day or two. You make something that almost looks like a goose, even if it is an odd shape. You like the feel of the metal in your hands, softening it, bending it and soldering the pieces together. And it keeps your mind off things.

Then you come to class in the second week to find a familiar figure at the front talking to the teacher. Diana. At the sight of her, your innards turn liquid. You have glimpsed her most days in the halls, but you haven't spoken to her since that day at your locker. She's a year older than you, in Grade Nine, so you shouldn't be in any of the same classes. Here she is, though, joining Metalwork 101 a week into the winter term.

In the halls, your eyes can flick away without acknowledgement. Here, you don't stand a chance. Mr. Holbrook gestures across the room, and Diana turns to see where he's pointing, which happens to be at your station. Not surprising. You're the only student with a station all to herself. Or you were. Diana's eyes and yours connect, flick away, and connect again.

Mr. Holbrook follows her across the room. "Kaya," he says, "Diana is joining the class today. Could you show her how to get started on her project, where to find the materials, et cetera?"

Diana ducks her head, breaking the tortured eye contact between the two of you. And you marshal yourself. You go through the motions that afternoon, but even as you instruct her on the proper safety procedures, you know that this is your last metalwork class. The whole experience is tainted now. It has become something other, something dark and dreadful. Diana has made it so. You have probably had the same effect on her, you think when it's over, as you watch her scurry from the classroom ahead of you.

That night, you climb out your bedroom window onto the roof of the foyer, wriggle down the fig tree right outside Mom's window, which is not easy in tight jeans and high heels, and you are away. It's later than usual, but surely they'll still be there, or one of them will. You jump off the bus across from the movie theatre on Granville, your bag slung casually over one shoulder, your jacket collar turned up against the drizzle, but you can see right away that there's no one there. You should have brought an umbrella. And a warmer coat.

It feels weird being outside in the city so late all by yourself. You can feel the eyes on you. And the danger. You think briefly about your own bed. Warm. Dry. Safe. Then you shake that off and march down the sidewalk. Most nights, they all sleep outside somewhere. You know that. It's just a matter of finding them.

The street grows darker, scarier. As you wait for the light at the first corner, cars seem to slow as they pass, faces leer.

A man approaches from one side, his gait slightly unsteady. "You all right, sweetheart?" he says, coming to a halt just as the light changes and you can cross.

"Yes," you say, stepping off the curb. "I'm fine." You look at your watch. It's past one. And you have no idea where to go. They could be anywhere. And the thought of these streets in the middle of the night, almost empty with who-knows-who watching out windows, out of alleys, frightens you.

"You don't look fine," a voice says, and you jump. The man is still there, right on your heels. All concern for your welfare, apparently.

A bus appears in the distance and you seize the chance, taking off at a high-heeled, tight-jeaned trot.

Climbing up fig trees is not as easy as slithering down. And Beth's window is too out of reach. The sliding door into the dining room opens easily enough, though. Sybilla swarms your legs, but her whines are quiet and Mom does not wake up.

Your own bed brings with it your own world. And that's the last place you want to be.

CHAPTER THREE

Kaya

In the morning, you wait for Michelle on the front steps of the school. *Come to school*, you beam out to her. *Come to school.* And she does.

As she approaches, you tell her, right off, "I need to get out of here."

Michelle draws close, her eyes round, hands running through her unwashed hair. Her eyes spark slightly. You aren't sure if that is fear or anger or what. And you don't care.

You repeat yourself. "I need to get out of here." You know that Michelle will want to help you; you also know that she'll know how.

If she is surprised, she does not show it. She glances from your small backpack to your even smaller purse to your eyes. "Now?" she says.

She doesn't ask why you don't go on your own. She seems to know that you want more this time, not just a bunch of lost kids hanging out on the street.

"This minute," you say. "I'm not walking into that school one more time."

"Do you have enough bus fare for me too?" she asks.

You nod. And she walks away from the school, obviously expecting you to follow. You do.

As the bus starts up the ramp onto the Granville Bridge, your heart picks up its pace, excitement zips through your jaw, your scalp, your gut.

On the other side, you press your face to the window and gaze at the kids leaning against the theatre wall, the dogs, the vendors' set-ups. You watch for the girl with the cat. If you see her, maybe you'll get off the bus right here. But you don't see her and the bus passes on. When it turns onto Hastings, your excitement is heightened by dread. You feel slightly sick. Are you really truly doing this?

Michelle chatters nervously, surprising you, but she doesn't say a word about where you are headed, and you don't ask. That might stop what you are doing somehow, and it seems like the only option, the only thing that will clear your head.

Even at ten thirty in the morning, Main and Hastings is a busy place. Busy on the sidewalk, that is. You try to look casual as you step off the bus, to swagger into the small crowd—mostly men—not cower close to the curb, but it's different here. Not like Granville at all. The people are older, mostly. They seem rougher, tougher. And there are more of them. Way more. And not mixed with the shoppers and the business people and the movie-goers. Despite your best efforts to appear calm, you feel yourself veer away from the bodies, arms close to your sides, purse clutched tight.

Michelle does not swagger or cower or clutch. She walks with a purpose that feels separate from yours. You have to trot to keep up at times, and you wonder if she even remembers that you are here.

"Michelle," you call out, but you don't want to draw attention to yourself and your voice does not reach her ears.

You walk faster, eyes on the ground, only to stumble into her where she waits outside a door between two buildings. On one side is a store, barred windows stacked with packages, on the other a hotel with grubby windows in which several faded plastic plants gather dust.

Michelle presses a buzzer, waits for an answering buzz and gives the door a good shove. It swings open onto a flight of stairs leading straight up. You look to the top and see a man peering down at you.

"Who's there?" he shouts.

"It's me," Michelle shouts back, her foot on the first step. "Michelle."

It takes him a moment to answer, and you wonder how she ever ended up here. Did someone bring her here just like she's bringing you, or did she find it all by herself?

At last he calls, "Come on up. Bring your friend."

He watches as you trudge your way up and looks you over as you get closer. He's a big guy—not old, you think— with scruffy black hair and a smile that eases your nerves, just a little. He holds out a hand and you take it; his grasp is warm and strong, and lingers just a bit longer than you like.

Michelle pushes past you and stops. "Is Marcos here?" she asks.

He shrugs, letting go of your hand. "That's all the hello

I get," he says. "Yes, he's here. Not in a great mood, I'd say, but here."

Michelle clatters off down the long hallway and through a door. The man turns back to you.

"I'm Jim, by the way. We'll just hang out here and give them a minute."

After a moment you say, "Kaya."

You hate standing on that scrappy carpet under a bald light bulb, while Michelle is in an unknown room with an unknown man. Jim rolls a cigarette on the spot and takes a few drags, his hacking, wet cough surrounding you with smoke. He doesn't question you, but he does look you over once or twice, his face blank.

Eventually he grunts and sets off and you follow him down the hall and through the door. The place is awful: not an apartment like you were expecting, but only a room with a sink in the corner. The stained mattress has no sheets on it, just a tangle of dirty quilts. The one small table is adrift in empty bottles and other garbage. The grubby window is open, but the air in the room stinks of cigarette smoke and dirty clothes and bodies and stale beer. It takes a few moments to take in all of this, however, because there is your friend, hunched on the bed, a boy at her side, and he's right in the middle of sticking a needle in her arm.

"Michelle, what are you . . . ?" You stop as you feel Jim behind you, hands on your shoulders. Michelle looks up, the spark in her eyes all gone.

You hear Jim take a breath to speak, but Michelle speaks first. "Hey, I got you here, didn't I? This is what you wanted, right?"

"Easy, kid," Jim says to you. "She's fine. Marcos is taking good care of her. He's known her for a long time."

Michelle lowers herself back onto the bed, and Marcos turns his attention to his own arm, showing no interest in you. Jim grasps your elbow. Hard.

"Let's grab a coffee," he says. "We'll talk."

You pull away from him and take two steps toward the bed. "No. I can't leave her. It's my fault she's . . ."

"She doesn't need you right now, honey. Can't you see how happy she is?"

You look down at her, lying across the bed now, head rolled to one side. *Happy* doesn't seem like the right word, but clearly she has done this before. And she was eager to bring you downtown because she wanted this. She wants to get high. She wants to escape her life. Well, you understand that. Though you'll never do what she's doing, no matter how much you want to forget.

You turn and look at Jim now and the word *pimp* leaps into your mind. Pimps and drugs go together, right? If you leave Michelle alone now, will men rape her? Is Jim going to take you somewhere all on your own where men can give him money for you? You feel frightened but also curiously detached at the thought. Kind of floaty. The instinct to protect Michelle is strong. The horror at what Michelle is doing is real. But the nervousness that clung to you all the way downtown on the bus is gone.

You smile. "Let's go!" you say to Jim.

The street is still filled with a milling-around crowd that confuses you. Jim keeps you close, though. He doesn't march off ahead like Michelle did. He turns in at a pair of windowless doors, pushes one open and stands aside to let you pass. The light inside is dim, but warm; the space is big and mostly empty. A woman calls hello from behind the bar. Two guys look up from a long table, a jug of beer between them.

Once you are seated, Jim leans back in his rickety plastic chair and signals to the waitress.

You squirm in your seat, breathing the smell of stale cigarettes and spilled beer, staring at the stained table. When you glance up, Jim's eyes are on you, and you look back down. He is nothing like any man you have ever met before. Not even . . . but you nix that thought quick.

The waitress runs a dirty cloth over the table and plunks down a jug and two big hard-plastic cups. Jim pours and drinks.

At last he speaks, slow, with a drawl. "So, did the girl bring you or did you bring her?"

You open your mouth. "I . . ."

He waits a moment, then says, "Not much of a talker, are you."

Your mouth snaps shut. You look at him, proving him right.

The answer to his question sits in your mind, heavy and sticky. *You* brought *her* and the reason for that is . . . The reason for that is . . .

Without planning it, you say, "My dad died."

He looks at you, brows raised. "Your dad died."

"Yes."

"And you're telling me that because . . . ?"

"I don't know. I guess I'm just really messed up."

Jim smiles briefly.

"Well," he says as he lifts his glass to his mouth, "I can help you out, if you want."

Your eyes stay on his face, trying to read it, to figure out what kind of help he is offering you. The same kind of *help* he gives Michelle, most likely. That isn't what you came here for. Is it?

The door to the bar opens and bodies and voices swirl in together. "Hey, Jim."

"Hey, kiddo."

"I've told you not to call me that. Who's this you've got here?"

The woman speaking is young and pretty. That's what you see first. Her hair is curly black and she has lots of it—it's kind of like yours. Her skin isn't far off your colour either, but everything else about her is different: her dress, skin-tight; her makeup and nails, perfect. She has broken away from her group to speak to Jim, and now she turns her attention on you.

"I'm, uh, I'm Kaya," you say, hating the catch in your voice. Here is somebody female who knows how to live in this world. You can't imagine this woman living in a nasty hotel room like Jim's, or knuckling under to a guy like him either.

"I'm Sarah," she says, pulling out a chair.

"Hey!" one of the women in the group calls out. She's tall, skinny, teetering on heels, gesturing broadly with long arms. "You're with us, Blackie."

You tense, but Sarah seems relaxed.

"Hang on to yourself," she calls back, grinning at her friend before she turns again to you.

"We don't need another hang-about," the woman in the group says, scowling now. She slings herself onto a chair and leans in to her companions. You can't hear what she says after that.

Jim puts his hand on your back, and Sarah looks down her nose at him.

"How long have you known Jim here?" she asks you.

You look at your watch, and she laughs. "Hands off, Jim," she says, her voice light, playful. "She's just a kid."

You straighten. "I am not. I'm . . . I'm . . ." But you can't bring yourself to lie to her. You *are* just a kid.

"See ya, Jim," Sarah says, and to you, "Come on, uh . . . what did you say your name was?"

"Kaya."

"Come on, Kaya."

You're happy to blow off Jim, but you balk at joining the others at their table.

"It's all right," Sarah says. "They won't bite." She laughs. "Right, guys? At least, they won't draw blood."

The scowler lets her eyes pass over you—scratchy, her gaze feels, while it lasts, which is only for a moment. Neither of the others looks up. You have to force yourself to sit.

After that, they ignore you for a while, and you start to relax and enjoy the energy. Cigarette smoke, raunchy jokes (*really* raunchy jokes), laughter, all of it swirls around you, warm and somehow comforting. You sip at a glass of beer and study them, one at a time. One is wearing worn-out sweats and runners with a T-shirt knotted at her waist; one is wearing boots with stiletto heels and a short skirt over bare legs and a low-cut top with ruffles around the neck. The scowler is wearing skinny jeans with those heels and a baggy tank top, her tattered leather jacket slung over her chair-back. Then there's Sarah in her stretchy dress.

Are they high? You have no clue. You don't think so. Are they prostitutes? You don't know that either, but you guess that the stilettos mean they are. Well, maybe not the one in the sweats.

As the glasses empty, the scowler turns her attention back to you. "So what's up with the kid?" she says to Sarah. "Is she your new little trainee? You going to raise her up? Be her grand protector?"

"Shut up, can't you?" Sarah says, looking sideways across the room at Jim, who moved tables when you abandoned him, joining the pair of guys who looked up when you entered the bar. "I was just getting her away from him. You know he chews them up and spits them out."

"He got me up and running," the woman with the ruffled blouse says. "And look at me."

You do, and you can't tell if she is being sarcastic or dead serious. She doesn't look great. She looks worn out. Worn through.

"He's no worse than anyone else," she adds.

The knotted T-shirt woman speaks then, but so quietly that all of you could have missed it if her words hadn't fallen into a moment of quiet between songs. "What about your Charlie?" That's what she says.

Sarah stands, pushing back her chair so fast it almost clatters to the floor. Jim and his friends look up, obviously eager for some drama, but "Fuck you" is all Sarah says as she grabs her coat and strides for the door. "Fuck you." She has to turn back when she's halfway there. "What's the matter with you, kid? Are you going to stay with *them*?" Then she's gone and you have to run to catch her in the morning drizzle.

"I'm worried about my friend," you say as you half jog along at her side down Hastings. "I left her in a hotel room with this young guy, Marcos. A friend of Jim's. She was shooting up."

Sarah stops. "Jesus," she says. "Well, that's what happens in Jim's hotel room. That's what happens in a lot of hotel rooms. That and other stuff." She stands still then, sheltering herself from the rain under an overhang, and asks you a few questions. At last she starts walking again, and you go back to jogging along at her side.

"I'm not sure if you can help her right this minute, Kaya," she says. "It sounds like she knows what she's doing. She took you there, right?"

You nod, thinking about that, about people leading other people into danger. Today wasn't the first time someone did that to you.

For a moment you are angry with Michelle, and it feels kind of good, this cloak of anger. But Michelle was perfectly safe at school just this morning, far from drugs and needles and all the other nameless dangers. You knew that she had been in trouble downtown. And you used that knowledge to get what you wanted. You might as well have walked right up to her at school and jabbed a needle into her yourself.

The anger slithers away, and your skin twitches at the shame that clings to you in its place.

As you walk, you snuggle into your coat and wonder how Sarah can stand her bare legs and thin fitted jacket in the cold damp. She doesn't look as gorgeous in broad daylight, you notice. Her clothes are a bit worn, a couple of sores show through her makeup, and her eyes are kind of dull. But her energy, her friendliness, trumps all that stuff. She seems to know everyone, or just says hello whether she knows them or not. You're not sure which, but it doesn't matter.

People say hello back, but Sarah never stops and she never introduces you to anyone.

You look and you don't look, not wanting to see the dirt, the misery, or, even worse, the fact that all that dirt and misery is attached to human beings. What are you doing here?

Then Sarah slows down. You are approaching a corner. PRINCESS AVENUE, the sign says. A corner store. And on the other side of Princess, the Union Gospel Mission down the block, and closer, two little grey houses, a matched set.

"This is where I get off," she says, pointing at the closest of the houses. "And this is where you get on."

You look at her, puzzled, and she grins. "On a bus, that is!" She seems awfully pleased at her own cleverness.

"But . . ." You aren't sure what to say, how to argue. "I . . . I just got here."

"That, Kaya, is the very best time to leave. Trust me," she says. Then, "I'm kind of busy here, actually."

She doesn't invite you into her house. She doesn't take you somewhere to talk. She doesn't tell you to come back sometime. She just ushers you toward the bus stop. You swallow thick hurt and take a step away from her.

"All right," you say, defeated. "I'll catch a bus."

"Do you have some money?"

You nod, even though all you have is a handful of coins in your pocket.

She pulls a crumpled ten-dollar bill from her minuscule purse. "Here," she says. "Get yourself a burger or a slice. And use the change to catch a bus home." She looks hard at you, almost glaring, and goes on. "Listen, Kaya," she says, "don't come back, okay?"

"Goodbye," you say, hating how tiny your voice is.

She looks into your eyes, and, almost as an afterthought, points again at the little house, its front step overgrown, its front windows boarded up. "If you ever need me, knock at the back door. Ask for Blackie." A pause, her eyes locked on yours. "Well, off you go, then." And she turns away.

Obediently you start walking back the way you came. When you look back, a few doors down, Sarah is gone. If only she had invited you in.

A bus is coming, but you ignore it. You don't have the right change anyway.

After an absence of an hour or so, Michelle is back in your head. She seemed to trust Marcos, but from what Sarah said, you know that she thought she was rescuing you from Jim. And what does that say about Jim's young friend?

Δ

It takes forever to find the building again. Your stomach grows demanding at a certain point and you pick up a couple of Chinese pork buns. You walk extra fast as you pass the hotel where Sarah found you with Jim. You don't want to run into him, or any of those women. Your stomach churns at the thought of facing the scowler all on your own.

Then you have to find the right bus stop—the one where

you and Michelle got off—and stand and remember. This way. No. That way. People look at you. One or two try to speak to you. But you put on your shell, the same one that's been working pretty well for you at school since Michelle rescued you from those girls—until Diana showed up, that is—a small self-assured smile, almost eye contact, but not quite, as if you have something important to do. A longish stride. Arms relaxed. Just past the first corner you have to stand again, retrace your steps. After a long search, you see the dusty plants and you are sure, though it's amazing how many dusty plastic plants you have had to examine before you find the right ones.

You stand and gaze at the buzzers. Five of them, grimy; the spots for names, empty. What should you do? Press them all? Your finger hovers, but before you commit, feet clatter down the stairs and Marcos himself barrels out the door almost right into your arms.

You move around him and stick your foot in the door before it swings shut. "Marcos," you say.

He looks at you, and you find yourself staring at his eyes; his pupils have disappeared. You resist the temptation to say *Anybody home?* and after a moment you see a glimmer of recognition.

"You're her friend," he says slowly.

"Yes," you say. "I need to get her now. We need to go."

"I don't think . . ." he begins, glancing back up the stairs, his eyes flicking nervously.

That's all you need to send you into the building. "I'll just get her myself," you call over your shoulder as you dash up the stairs. Maybe he'll go away. Maybe she's in there all by herself. Maybe. This isn't safe, you think. You should call the police. Or Michelle's mother. Her foster mother, that is. And you wonder for a moment what she has been through in her life. Anyway, you're not calling anyone. You're going in.

Marcos rattles up the stairs after you, but you get to the room before he does and the handle turns when you try it. You push it open and stand in the doorway, adjusting to the dim light. The room looks much as it did earlier, except that a second figure is in the bed, making a hump in the quilts. You don't have to look to be pretty sure it's Jim, snoring away. Michelle, on the other side of the bed, is kind of propped up against the wall. Marcos stops behind you.

"You can't be here," he says slowly, quietly so as not to disturb the hump.

You ignore him and step forward. Michelle is awake, you realize, as you see her head shift, her gaze lift, peer out. "I'm here," you whisper, hoping she will hear, hoping Jim will not.

At the bottom of the bed, you stop, lean forward, grab a foot. "Let's go, Michelle," you say. "Let's get out of here."

Slowly, slowly, she loosens herself from a quilt and wriggles your way. You turn your eyes away when you realize she has no clothes on her bottom half, and scrabble around on the floor for her pants. You get her onto her feet and into her pants and turn toward the door. Marcos is long gone. The heap on the bed shifts once and you both freeze, but all that emerges is a snorty snore.

Nobody stops you on the stairs, on the street, at the bus stop. Your left arm tight around Michelle's waist, you jam coins into the slot on the bus until one then two transfers pop out at you.

"Get a move on," the driver says. "There's people on this bus with somewhere to go."

Your head rears up and you sneer, but Michelle tugs at you. "Just get the tickets," she says.

So you do, relief at the sound of her voice washing away your anger. The two of you teeter to the back, giggling as you bump into people, grabbing at each other and the backs of seats for balance. You swing into the best seat, the one at the rear, nothing but bus behind you. Michelle has the window, and you sit back a bit and look at her. Is she all right?

She smiles kind of shyly. Her eyes look funny, like Marcos's but more so. She seems swirly, mushy, somehow. But she leans into your shoulder and you feel the contact all the way through you. It's real, meant. You manage a bit of a lean back.

"Thanks for coming to get me," she says.

"I couldn't just leave you there," you say, remembering that you did exactly that and that you even considered going home without her. You look her over again. "Are you all right?" you ask. "That man, Jim, was there." You pause. "In the bed." You want to add, *and you were naked.* But you can't say those words. "Do you . . . do you need to go to the hospital?"

She leans back as you speak, her eyes sliding shut, her head lolling.

A man looks at her from the sideways seats and rage crackles through your forearms and into your fingertips. You tighten all the muscles in your face, flare your nostrils and give him your best sneer, even better than the one you were lining up for the bus driver. Then you turn, reach out and give Michelle a shake. She moans quietly, shakes her head and sinks deeper into her druggy's sleep.

She sleeps the rest of the way, while your thoughts grind your brain down to a pulp. The light is fading by the time you steer her off the bus. You see her to her door, even wait while she walks through it. After that, you are all alone with yourself.

Your own house is only three blocks away. You wander down Eleventh and turn at the corner, one foot in front of the other. It would be nice to get home where it's warm. Your bed is there, unmade perhaps, but clean and sheeted. The fridge is there. The TV is there.

And Mom and Beth. Looking at you, thinking about you, worrying about you. You stop and look back the way you came, toward that bus stop. You think of Sarah. Her straight back. Her strong shoulders. Yes, she told you to go home, but if home is supposed to be so great, why doesn't she go to hers? She's obviously sorted out a way to live downtown and keep a spring in her step. If you told her . . . If you explained . . .

Your transfer is still good.

The bus passes you just as you reach Tenth Avenue, sending a wall of water over the curb. Three people at the stop down the street start putting down their umbrellas and shuffling forward. You pick up your pace. Perfect timing! Then, it seems as if the bus and the people speed up and you slow down. If you shout, you think, it will come out all stretchy and weird. In an instant, the bus has swallowed the people and their umbrellas. It pulls away. You wave and shout, your voice sharp and ordinary—not stretchy at all—to no effect.

"Fucking bus driver," you snarl. If you were a forty-year-old white lady, he'd wait. No question. You look back up the street. No bus. Your body shivers. You feel like slapping it. A little rain and it goes all to pieces.

By the time the next bus comes, your transfer will be worthless. You upend your purse onto the sidewalk and examine the coins you have left: three dollars and forty-seven cents. That will get you on the bus and leave you with less than a dollar once you get down there.

Even with that knowledge, even with the rain dribbling down your neck, even with your body's shakes and shivers, you stand there. A man strides past, his muttered "Excuse me" code for *What are you doing standing in the middle of the sidewalk in the rain?*

"Fuck you," you mutter at his back, not loud enough for him to hear. Your teeth crash together, chattering, on the *you*. You almost stomp your foot as you turn and head for home.

Beth is on her way down the stairs when you open the door, and she stops on the third step from the bottom, eyes widening in relief. "She's here!" she calls, and Mom comes charging out of the kitchen.

You close the door behind you and shrink against it for a moment. Then, "Yeah, I'm here," you say sharply to your mother as you shove your way past Beth and head up the stairs. "I'm here, and I need some dry clothes."

"When Beth came home alone, I called the school," Mom is saying as you close your bedroom door. "They said you—"

You shock yourself a little with your own rudeness, but what else can you do? If you have to stay in their company for one fraction of a second, a fraction of a fraction of a second, you will scream words that will make their ears bleed. Better this way.

A small knock interrupts you minutes later as you strip off your wet clothes. The door inches open. It's Beth.

"Are you all right?" she says as you bound across the room and slam the door on her.

"I'm fine, Beth. Fine," you say through the closed door. "Just leave me alone. Please!"

There. That should do it. You even said *please*. Why are they freaking out so much anyway? It's not even suppertime. You've been away way longer than this.

You pull on a flannel nightshirt and huddle on your bed, drawing the quilt around yourself, letting the warmth seep in. As your body stops shaking, hunger asserts itself. Why, oh why, didn't you stash some food in your room? And where's Sybilla?

When you look at your clock, you're shocked that it says four thirty. It seems impossibly early and impossibly late, both at the same time. You doze a bit. Wake again. Six o'clock. After that, you lie awake, watching that clock and waiting. For what, precisely, you can't say.

Over and over, your mind takes you back to the sight of Michelle, scrambling, bottomless and barely conscious, out of that bed. Diana wanders into your mind. It takes all your concentration to get her out again.

Not long after that, your hunger turns ravenous. Pork buns long gone. At six thirty, Mom taps on your door.

"Supper's ready, honey." Long pause. "Would you like me to bring you up a plate?"

Your stomach growls, so loud that you can hear it. "No," you snarl. "Can't you just leave me alone?" Why can't she ever, ever just leave you alone?

You slide onto the floor and dig into an ancient toy chest full of old dolls and dress-up clothes, reaching underneath everything and feeling around until you come up with a little girl's diary complete with lock. Scissors. Scissors. It takes you a minute, but you find those too, and *snip*, the piece that holds the book closed is no more.

You flip through quickly, looking for the blank part, not interested in reading your nine-year-old drivel. Not interested at all. Blank page found, you forget your grumbling gut for a while, you forget that strange and terrible trip downtown, as you create a list, a catalogue, of your sister's various stupidities.

At last, at eight o'clock, the house settles, grows quiet, and you shove the diary right back where you found it and head downstairs. Sybilla rises from the carpet. You sink to your knees, wrap your arms around her and bury your face in her fur, and remember. One sob, big and deep. She wriggles against you. She has love to spare and she knows nothing of the deep dark dirty places inside of you. Another sob, this one even deeper.

"Kaya?"

Beth has followed you down the stairs. She is standing behind you, her path to the kitchen blocked by the pair of you: happy dog, sad girl. She looks desperate. Terrified.

You feel the skin pull back from your teeth; your eye sockets clench.

Beth stands for a long moment looking at you. Then she turns and runs back upstairs.

In the kitchen, you stand in front of the fridge, rip the plastic wrap off a bloody hunk of grilled steak and devour it, almost without chewing. You find a bag of cookies in the cupboard and take it upstairs, but the meat in your belly is all you need.

Sleep comes then, easy.

CHAPTER FOUR

Kaya

The next morning, you get up and get ready for school. Mom bustles in the kitchen, while Beth sits at the table, hair in her face, eating an oversized bowl of bran flakes and granola. After a bit, Mom goes to wait in the car. The drive to school is silent. You can feel Mom wanting to speak, to find the words that will keep you in school this day, and the next.

You feel sorry for her, almost, and when she pulls over in front of the school, you lean into the front seat and kiss her on her soft pink cheek. Her breath flies out of her in a whoosh, and her hand comes back around and grasps your head. You pull away, and the moment is over.

Beth is already standing outside the car by the time you get out, waving kind of awkwardly at Jane and Samantha, who are waiting on the school steps. She turns back to you before she waddles off. "You be here today at three," she says. And if Beth can be fierce at all, she's fierce now.

You grin. "When have I ever let you down?" you say, your voice bright and crisp.

She stares. You know she wants to say, *Every day of your life, since the day you came.* You imagine the tip of her tongue all bloody from where she's biting it. She just can't say something like that, no matter how much she longs to.

You drop the act. "I'll be here," you say. And you will be. You can't go back downtown today anyway. Not without a bit of cash.

The day is long, though, and so is the next one. Michelle does not show up at school and you wonder about that. Has she gone back down there? If she has, is that all your fault?

Diana does show up at school, of course. Even though you have dropped the metalwork class, the two of you keep running into each other. And every time, acid swirls right up your throat. She seems to have the same reaction, because she turns away as fast as you do. The two of you dart all over the place to avoid each other.

The third night, you steal forty dollars from Mom's wallet and twenty from Beth's babysitting stash in her underwear drawer. She doesn't babysit a whole lot, but she's not good about getting her money into the bank, so she usually has some tucked away. You may have done some shoplifting last year, but you've never stolen from your family before. You've only ever taken a bit of change from Mom's purse for the bus. And you have permission to do that.

After supper, you slip out the front door and run all the way to Tenth. This time, the bus cooperates. It ought to: you have the schedule all figured out. You'll be at Sarah's door at about seven. Who, you wonder, will be on its other side?

It turns out that you don't have to go to her door at all. She's getting out of a big white car as you get off the bus.

It turns the corner and drives right past you, so you see the man behind the wheel. You see his tidy hair, his suit jacket. You see the child seat in the back. You feel sick.

You stand back and wait until after she turns down Princess Avenue. You don't want her to know that you saw her get out of that car. You want to un-know it yourself.

"Sarah!" you say, jogging to catch up to her, hoping your voice sounds confident and grown-up.

She turns and looks at you. Her eyes seem a bit vacant somehow. It takes her a moment to focus. "You look familiar," she says, "but I don't . . ."

"I'm Kaya," you say. "Remember?"

"Oh, yes. You're that kid," she says. She has come to a halt on the sidewalk. "I told you to go home and stay there." She looks you over, pushes a hand back through her hair. "Come on. We're going for a walk."

She walks strong and tall, even though she's actually pretty short. She seems oblivious to the fact that she's wearing thigh-high boots with spike heels and a short skirt that shows some skin way up at the top of those boots. Everyone looks as you pass; even people slumped in doorways look. Often they call out hello. Sometimes the hello isn't nice, but mostly it is. You wrestle with a mix of embarrassment and pride as you follow her. She takes you over a viaduct, eventually, a bridge over a railway that circles around and leads right into a great big park on the water. Street lights brighten the path ahead. Huge cranes tower in the harbour. Even in the dark, the slight drizzle, the water sparkles on your right. Downtown, all lit up, straight ahead.

Sarah leads you to the swings in the playground. No

street lights here, so the playground equipment, dimly lit, feels lonely, abandoned.

You hesitate. How old does she think you are? But she plunks herself down on the middle swing. "Here," she says, kicking a leg up toward you. "Pull. These things are killing me."

You stare and then obey, pulling one long shiny boot from a leg, then the other, and dropping them on the grass beside her purse. She pumps back and forth, her legs strong, her body reaching for the sky.

"Come on," she shouts. "It's amazing!"

And you do, shaking the small puddle off the strip of rubber. You push off, lean back, straighten your legs, and forget the left-behind damp seeping through your jeans as you aim your face at the dark wet above. The two of you look at each other when you are both as high as you can go, flying. And you laugh, loud, together. Your chest expands with joy. Then she starts to slow herself down. Soon the two of you are weaving your swings back and forth, scuffing your feet in the damp sand.

"Why are you here?" she asks, her gaze intent on the ground.

"I can't be at home," you say, not pausing, just saying.

"Why not?"

"It's horrible there," you say, and your mind flashes to Mom's loving hand in your hair, to Sybilla's big furry body. Horrible?

She looks at you then, and you feel her see right inside you; you shrink under her gaze.

"I don't belong there," you say, too fast. "I belong here."

"No, you don't," she says, and adds after a moment, "This is not a good place to be."

"You're here," you say.

She is silent for a long, long time. Then she says, "Something bad happened to me. When I was little. And I never told my mom and dad. I should have. I really, really should have told. I should have stayed."

"That's not me," you say, big and strong, and you stop scuffing the ground, start swinging again. You need to move. "That's not me."

"I don't believe you," she says. Then, "Look. Look at the cats."

They are coming up from the beach: three, no, four, no, five cats, heading across the grass in the dark. They are silent, stealthy, like ghosts. Sarah laughs softly.

"Here, kitties," she calls. "Here, kitties."

You grunt and start pumping, driving yourself up into the air again, watching. Sarah goes quiet, watching too. You let yourself slow and come to a stop beside her.

The cats circle, not coming close enough to touch. Even in the dark, you can see the matted fur and bald patches on one, the jagged ear on another. A third meows, big and demanding—hungry—like no sound Coco has ever made in her life.

"We've got nothing for you, cats," Sarah says. "On your way now."

They obey, wandering away, across the park, and Sarah leans over to pull her boots back on. "Let's go," she says. "I'm putting you on a bus. Again."

She leads the way back to the path, and stops in front of

a big stone surrounded by bushes, lit by a tall lamp opposite. First you notice the candles and the flowers gathered in the wet dirt in front. Then your gaze travels upward to the words engraved in the stone.

THE HEART HAS

IN HONOR OF THE SPIRIT OF THE PEOPLE
MURDERED IN THE DOWNTOWN EASTSIDE.
MANY WERE WOMEN AND MANY WERE NATIVE
ABORIGINAL WOMEN. MANY OF THESE CASES
REMAIN UNSOLVED. ALL MY RELATIONS.

ITS OWN MEMORY

DEDICATED JULY 29, 1997

You read the words twice. A third time. Anger flutters inside you, along with fear and confusion. "Why are you showing me this?" you ask.

Sarah shrugs, gestures toward the words again.

You read them one more time.

At last she speaks. "Those women. They could be you. They could be me." She digs around in her tiny purse, pulls out a lighter, leans down and lights one of the candles, positioning it under a plastic flower to protect it from the damp. Then she turns and leads the way up the path onto the viaduct. She doesn't say much on the walk back to Princess. And neither do you.

With Hastings in sight, you pass the little grey house that Sarah pointed out to you. A man comes barrelling down the narrow path between that house and the next. He's big, hunched over, kind of. And mad. Mad at Sarah.

"Where the hell you been?" he shouts as he approaches. He pauses, as if at a loss for other words. "Where the hell you been?" he repeats, and his hand shoots out and grabs Sarah around the upper arm.

"Hey!" she says sharply, and you pick up your pace, putting a few strides between yourself and the pair of them. "Let go of me, Charlie. I've just got one thing to do and I'll be . . ."

He wrenches at her then, and she turns on him, yanking her arm free. "I said, I've just got one thing to do." She strides after you, ignoring his repeated orders to "Get back here."

"Who's he?" you say, though you guess, of course.

"That's just Charlie. He goes off the deep end now and again. Pay attention. We are going to get you on a bus. You're going to go home, and you're going to stay there. Do you understand?"

You do not. Understand, that is. Even as Sarah is saying it, you are thinking about the money in your pocket. You are thinking about how soon you can come back. After all, you know where to come to now. You know where she lives. Charlie is a bit scary, but she seems to know how to handle him.

Δ

Less than a week passes before you get off another bus right at the corner of Princess and Hastings. You stand on the sidewalk for a moment in front of the house: 396 Princess Avenue. You gaze up at the boards on the windows, down at the dead weeds that crawl across the cracked cement steps, at the icy remnants of snow.

Uncertain, you creep round to the back, up half a dozen wooden steps onto a falling-down landing. Once again, it is seven o'clock. Dark. Everything sodden. Bits of grey snow cling to patches of earth and to the railing, but the snow doesn't stick to the wet rotted boards beneath. Melt drips off the edge of the roof and collects in puddles on the expanse of gravel between the pair of small grey houses and the lane.

You stand on the landing, your hands at your sides. Eventually, you will raise one hand and knock. Eventually, you will. And when you do, maybe Sarah will answer. Maybe she will invite you in and be kind to you again.

Maybe she will not answer. Maybe that man will. That big crumbling man who grabbed her arm.

You raise your hand and knock. Three knocks. Silence. Four knocks. More silence. You force your fist to pound instead of knock. "Hello?" you call. "Hello!" you shout.

"Who's there?" comes a voice through the wood. A man's voice.

You could still run now, but you don't. "It's me, Kaya. Sarah's friend," you call back. Then you remember. "Blackie," you add.

The door opens a crack, revealing a strip of face; an eye peers out, squinting into the dark. You can't tell if the eye recognizes you, but the door opens, revealing the body attached to the eye. It's that man, the one who grabbed.

You see no sign of Sarah, but you can't very well turn and run now.

"Come on in," he says. And you do.

"I'm, uh, I'm looking for Blackie," you say.

"Yeah?"

It's hard to know what to reply to that. You nod. And look around. You're standing in what passes for a kitchen and you don't like what you see. This mess, this brokenness, this dirt are not what you imagined for Sarah, the strong Sarah, the together Sarah. A mixing bowl lies on its side on the counter dribbling something that might be chocolate pudding onto the cracked linoleum. The window above the sink is boarded over, and the sink is half full of dishes not quite covered in scummy water. A scrawny kitten rubs itself against your leg. You start, and bend over in relief to run your hand along its bony spine.

"You can wait in there," the man, whose name you can't remember, says. He's pointing into a room off the kitchen.

You look hopefully toward the other doorway, which must lead into the living room, but he is sending you into a bedroom instead.

"No," you say, hating how weak your voice sounds. "I'll . . ."

His voice grows stern, impatient. "You'll wait in there or you'll get out," he says.

The better of the two choices is obvious, but you don't take it. In the room, a man sprawls in a broken easy chair, head back, apparently unconscious. High, you guess. And a woman sits at a small desk, intent on what she's doing. She does not look up. When you see what she has on the desk in front of her, something runs through you, skull to toes. It's horror, you tell yourself, but you know it's excitement, really.

The man—you remember his name now: it's Charlie—is right behind you. "Sit. There," he says, his hands pressing on your arms. And he plunks you on the edge of the bed, where you perch, rigid, and watch the woman's every movement.

After a while, she looks up and meets Charlie's eyes. He nods. "Hold out your arm," she says to you.

You look out into the kitchen, where the door you came through remains closed. Still no sign of Sarah. You look up at Charlie, but he is fiddling with some things on the desk and does not glance your way. And you look at the woman. She waits, her hand extended.

"Your arm," she says again.

The excitement takes you over then. Anticipation. Your arm and what she is about to do with it are keys to this place, this life, these people. Michelle couldn't handle it, but you are stronger than she was. Sarah seems to manage just fine with this stuff. And you need it, whatever it is, not just to belong here, but to get away from there. Mom and Beth don't understand you. Diana lurks at school, tainting the place. Michelle just makes you feel guilty. And everywhere at home, everywhere, are those memories. These people, here, have memories too. Here, pasts are understood with hardly a word spoken.

Besides, if you don't like it, you don't have to do it again.

You hold out your arm.

Moments later, you are puking in the garbage can while Charlie grumbles.

"What are you, a first-timer?" he asks.

You're in no condition to answer him, and couldn't care less. A little vomit is a small price to pay for the glory that is you with that stuff in your veins. Happiness floods your whole body, happiness and strength and clarity. Later you'll remember that you spent your first heroin trip lying on a filthy bed in a room full of strangers, reeking of your own puke, but while you're on that trip, none of that matters. All your problems—all of them—have slipped away like smoke. Who cares what happened in the past? Who cares who's dead and who's alive? Who cares what anyone thinks about anything? Not you, that's for sure.

Sometime later . . . you have no idea when . . . Sarah is there. "She's just a kid," she's saying. "Why did you do this?

"I'm not a kid," you mumble, but the words are hard to say. They come so slowly. Like molasses, you think, though really, you have never seen molasses, so how can you know how it comes? And, anyway, you don't want to talk with Sarah. You just want to lie here and revel in what you're feeling.

More time passes. The glory fades, not all at once, but eventually it is gone. Life feels flat. You turn onto your side on the bare mattress, and look down to find your nose inches from a stain that could be blood or puke or something even worse. Disgust worms into your belly and twists its way everywhere. You're alone in the room, and you heave yourself to your feet, aim yourself at the door.

Behind the disgust, though, or riding it maybe, is knowledge: scary, precious, heady, dangerous knowledge. If you want to, you can feel that glory again.

Sarah sweeps back into the room then, Charlie right behind her. And she's angry. Really angry. Why? you wonder. After all, she does this stuff every day. It's her life: earning the money for it, doing it, earning the money for it, doing it. That life might not be all that she ever hoped for, but she has no business ordering you out of it.

It's four o'clock in the morning, too late for buses. Charlie hustles you out of his room and shuts himself up inside. The others, the woman who ordered you to hold out your arm, and the man on the nod in the chair are gone. You stand in the kitchen, every bit of you lost. Sarah glares at you.

"This way," she says finally, and ushers you to a room at the front of the house. "You can sleep in there. Lock the door behind you."

And you do. You have no idea where she spends the night. You don't sleep, though, at least not for a long time. The kitten scratches on the door after a bit. You let it in, and spend what feels like hours stroking it while you turn the darkness that is your life over and over inside your head.

In the morning, when you venture out of the room, Sarah's there. She waits while you use the filthy bathroom to pee and then thrusts coins into your palm and virtually strong-arms you onto the bus.

Δ

But you go back. And back again.

And find Jim. After all, you can't keep going to Sarah's house. Jim doesn't send you home. You hold out your arm, and he seems happy to shoot you full of drugs. Then, when you are nodding off blissfully on that filthy bed of his, he crawls on top of you. You come back to yourself later, leaning against the wall just like Michelle did, your pants on the floor, Jim a hump in the bed. But, unlike Michelle, no one is waiting to take you away. You creep from the bed, dress and look around for Jim's wallet, but he is still wearing his pants, and it's not like you can rifle through his pockets when they are still on his body.

Turns out, he expects you to do more than put up with him on top of you to earn your way.

And so.

The first time is a man in a room. He is big and old; his pale flesh jiggles; he sweats and he smells. And he pays Jim, not you. You hate them both, but you hate yourself more. You smile and shimmy and giggle and make jokes and all the other stuff that you somehow know is expected, and it's like how they say people go out of their bodies when they are in hospital dying, how they look down on themselves. You watch yourself with the old fat man, and you are totally grossed out, but you're doing it just the same. Like you were born to it or something.

Part of what grosses you out is how easy it is, how your body just does it, how nothing in you resists, despite your feelings. Born to do it. Bad, through and through.

The first time with that man, you watch his chest as he moves up and down above you. It is loose and wobbly, and sprouts long grey hairs. You look at every detail carefully, filing it away. You listen to the sounds he makes—grunts and pants, mostly. It seems to take a lot of effort.

As long as you keep your attention on the man, you can keep it off yourself.

Δ

You don't stick with Jim for long, though.

It turns out he isn't the type to hold on, to come after a

girl. He kind of rolls along with things. Lucky for you. You wake on the edge of drug sickness late one afternoon to find yourself alone in that grubby bed in that tiny, stifling room.

You sit up, disgusted by your own skin, itchy and grey from neglect, by the taste in your mouth, sour, like dead things are rotting in your gut. You push the filthy quilt off the bed and look around, really look.

Imagine Beth seeing this. Smelling it. Or, even worse, Jane. *Why would anyone live like this? Ever?* they would say. And you. You. You have a home to go to. Beth would cry. Jane would sniff through her pointy little nose.

But.

There is something right about being here. About you being here. Maybe not right here in this room, but here in this place. Slowly, you slide from the bed, pull on clothes that have not been washed in days. How many days? A jolt runs through your body. Mom will be frantic. The jolt is followed by longing, deep and wide.

You stuff your few belongings into your purse, find a quarter in a puddle of beer on the battered table, run down the stairs, out the door, and stand blinking in the late-afternoon sun. Pay phones are rare in this neighbourhood, but you find one at last, plug in the quarter and pray that Mom and Beth will both be where they should be. Out.

You gasp at the sound of Mom's voice, relieved that it's canned, glad to hear it, and sad, so sad. "Hi, Mom," you say. "I'm okay. Don't worry about me. I'll call again soon."

There. That's done.

So. You aren't going home and you aren't going back to Jim's. You turn toward Princess Avenue, but that's not right either. Sarah will just shove you onto the first bus that comes along.

"You look lost," a voice says in your ear.

You jump, take a step away. Mom's voice lingers in your head, overlaid with this woman's words.

The woman is wearing a short skirt, heels and a tank top, with a ratty sweater overtop. Her dirty hair is kind of puffed up around her head, and her makeup looks like she shovelled it on in the dark. Her eyes are deep and black, and she's jittery—that's from the drugs, you know. You suspect she is much younger than she looks.

"I . . . I need to make some money," you say. Really? Are you really going to do that? Stand on a corner? "And I don't know which corners are okay." Yes. Apparently you are.

"Did you just come in on the bus or something?"

"No," you say. "I . . ."

She interrupts, her voice grown darker, raspier. "Well, you can't work here."

You blink hard against the tears that fill your eyes, back away, turn and start walking.

Home, you think. You could go home right this minute. You could.

As if in answer, a bus rumbles toward you. You watch it approach, roll to a stop, swallow three passengers, spit out two others and rumble away.

Two of the tears manage to get onto your cheeks; you grit your teeth and rub at your face. No. You are not going home.

Pushing your shoulders back, you collect your thoughts. You need a corner where no one will tell you to get lost. All you have to do is find one. And if you can get some money, you can get some drugs and you can feel good again, maybe not as good as that first time, but still. You can feel better, and you can get yourself a room of your own. You can get by without Jim. You can. On you walk, turning the next corner off Hastings, crossing Princess quickly when you come to it.

Twenty minutes later, you think you have found a spot, a corner on Cordova; there's traffic, but it's away from houses and apartments. Factories or some such all around. A fine drizzle is falling, like always in Vancouver in March. Sickness rises in your belly, a mix of withdrawal and fear.

You need money. You need a fix. You need a place to stay. You need a washing machine and a dryer. A shower. A meal.

You need a friend.

First order of business: cash. You hitch your skirt up high around your waist, nip your shirt in and tie a knot in it, sling your purse across your back and step up to the curb. The light on the next corner turns green and cars surge in your direction. *Shimmy*, you tell yourself, and you do. Just a bit. The cars roll on, and you have to leap back to avoid being splashed.

Next light, more cars. This time, a window slides down. "Whore!" you hear, just as you see the faces—teenage boys—and feel the sting as the pennies they throw strike your hip and your leg. You stand for a moment, empty. Not even angry.

The light changes again and you step up. You see the cars, leap once more out of the spray. You don't see the car coming to a stop on the side street. The guy has to lean across the passenger seat and shout out the open window at you. "Hey! Need a ride?"

You almost call back no, before you realize what he means.

Sliding into the passenger seat and pulling the door shut against the racket and the rain, you find yourself in an almost-silent space, heavy with the smell of stale cigarette smoke. You take one look at the man—grey-haired, glasses, eyes vague and sad, and maybe sort of kind; he's dressed for an office job of some sort—and fix your eyes on your lap.

The silence grows. Then, a little breath, a huff. Annoyance?

"So," he says, "where to and how much?"

You shrink into the seat, shoulders rounding forward, and force your eyes up to meet his once again. He doesn't look sad or vague now. And certainly not kind. He looks angry. And you, you have not one single idea what to say.

"Wherever you usually go," you mumble finally. "And thirty dollars."

The rest of the conversation, though it only lasts a few seconds, actually hurts, like it hacks off bloody chunks of you. But you get through it. He puts the car in drive. And off you go.

He slows down half a block away, turns into an alley, stops and puts the car in park. Then he takes money out of his wallet, puts it in the cup-holder between you and unzips himself. He gives another impatient huffing breath as you sit, still frozen, looking at him sideways. Then his right hand comes up, grabs your head and pulls you toward him. With his other hand, he pulls his penis out of his pants.

His is not your first, not at all. It's not the first time you've felt an insistent hand in your hair. But something about this moment gathers all those other moments up in your mind. Revulsion rumbles through you, starting deep, deep down. Bile gushes up into your throat, and you retch. Instantly, his hand flees your scalp. He leans away, scrabbling at his crotch. In one movement you turn away, open the door and half roll out of the car. Hands against the nearby wall, you vomit. Behind you, you hear him swear, you hear the car door slam shut, you hear the car drive away.

And there you are, alone, in an alley, in the rain, your pockets still empty and your stomach still emptier. The vomiting has cleared your mind, though the nausea will not leave you until you get yourself a fix. That is what all this is for, you remind yourself, that and a roof over your head that is not Jim's. Or your mother's. You can do this.

You straighten your back and start off, stepping up to the curb whenever a car passes. Within half an hour you have slid into your second car of the day. This time you keep your head up, you speak first, you even raise your price. And you do not gag. Not once.

You end the day with enough money for that fix and for a meal, and you pay a woman the few dollars you have left to sleep on the floor of her room. You lie there, wrapped in a dirty blanket, listening to drunken shouting, doors banging and endless traffic, and feel withdrawal easing its way back into your system, taking hold. You'll wake up sick. And out you will go to do it all again.

Δ

That woman helps you out, though, the next day, and others do too, in exchange for some of your money. You mention keeping an eye out for Jim, and "I started off with Jim too," a scraggly young woman tells you, sneering as she speaks. She coughs hard before she goes on. "He can be rough, but he's not the sort to come after you. A lot of them do. Once they've got you, you're stuck."

These women aren't always nice about it, but they show you the ropes, how to work the street, where to stand, how to keep off others' toes. They don't ask a lot of questions, and you are grateful.

Sarah is different. Sarah won't let you work her corner, but not because she's guarding her turf. She seems to be protecting you. Or trying to. If Sarah had her way, you wouldn't work at all. "Go home, kid," she says to you every time she sets eyes on you.

You still like seeing her, though, even though you ignore her advice.

Most days, "Hi, Blackie," you call out, grinning, using her nickname, lifted up by her energy, the gorgeous boots, the wide smile in the perfectly made-up face.

"Hey, kid, I'm working here," Sarah replies, but there's no meanness in her voice. "Get a move on."

Δ

One afternoon in spring, as you walk away down Princess, you find yourself turning and looking back just in time to see Sarah's foot disappear into a slick silver car. You make a mental note of the look of the car, though you're at the wrong angle to see the plate. A car like that could mean a good haul, you think. It's been a while since you had a john with real money, but you are having a good day.

You wander through Oppenheimer Park in the sunshine, heels clicking on the cement, hips swishing just like those other girls', insides gathering together into something strong, something fabulous, something everybody wants. You light a cigarette to complete the picture, cough a little on the first puff, watch the smoke whoosh into the air.

You suck in deep on the cigarette as you turn into a lane. The ball of fabulousness in your gut softens. You feel a bit like puking. But on you go.

CHAPTER FIVE

Beth

"I'm not leaving you home on your own," Mom says. "You can stay with Jane or Samantha or come with me."

"What about Kaya?"

"Kaya is gone."

"But what if she comes home?"

Mom's face is red and blotchy. She hacks at a carrot as if she were executing it. Veins stand out on the backs of her hands. "It's been weeks, Beth. Weeks. I've been out looking. I've talked to the police. I don't believe she's coming home just now."

Mom doesn't know that. She can't. But she isn't cancelling her trip. She's leaving the house locked and empty. Sybilla is with a friend till Sunday, Coco will have to fend for herself.

"I should stay home in case she comes," I say, again. We have been having this same conversation over and over again for more than a week.

"No."

I don't say one word to her on the whole four-hour drive to Kamloops. She puts an audio book on, a mystery set in the Victorian period, but I can't even stand to share sound waves with my mother. I plug myself into my own music, and sneak my way through an enormous bag of wine gums that I have hidden in my coat pocket.

Kaya is just a kid and she is lost. Mom is her mother and she is driving away. And I . . . I am a greedy pig. I finger the roll of fat around my middle, and think about how, when I look in the mirror, what pass for my breasts kind of sit on top of all that fat. Gross. I went on a diet once, before Dad died. I lost twelve pounds. He actually commented on how good I looked. But jelly beans and ice cream have appealed to me a lot more than counting calories since then.

The conference is at a lodge, a sprawling wooden structure, all logs and homespun tackiness. I pick the bed nearest the window, and plunk down my bag and myself.

"I'll just hang out here," I say, and Mom frowns and goes off to register for the conference on her own.

Why is she so upset? I'm here, aren't I? And it's not like I'm going to be going along with my mother to a bunch of sessions on childhood trauma and sexual abuse. If she's angling for a career change, I don't know why she doesn't choose something a tad more cheerful.

The moment the door closes, though, I wish I were out there with her. I imagine the phone at home ringing and ringing with only Coco to hear it. Kaya trapped, bruised and bleeding, begging us to come to her. I curl up in a ball on the bed. Where is Kaya right this minute? Is somebody hurting her?

I sit up, teeth gritted. How could Kaya go there anyway? And then go back? And not call? It's not like Mom was beating her or anything. What's her problem? And how can Mom drive away into the mountains and leave her daughter to her fate?

Later I follow Mom into the dining hall a little worried about how I'm going to get out again. There's a speaker after dinner, but I'm sure not going to sit around and listen to somebody drone on and on about all the miseries of childhood. I've got enough of my own to deal with, thank you very much!

I'm happy to see that it's a buffet, at least, and the food is good, though the man who slices the roast beef isn't generous. The dessert table is huge, three massive cakes at its centre, one chocolate, one layered with whipped cream and fruit, and one a plain cheesecake with three choices of sauce.

I'm still in the middle of a slab of the chocolate cake when a hush falls over the room. A woman has appeared at the lectern. Behind her another woman, elegantly dressed, waits to be introduced.

Mom turns her chair around so she can see. Waiters float through the room pouring coffee and removing plates.

"Welcome to Kamloops," the woman at the lectern says.

I put down my fork. "I'll see you later," I whisper in Mom's ear, and get only a fraction of a nod in reply. Mom's eyes stay trained on the front.

Sneaking out is awkward. Actually, it hardly qualifies as sneaking, since our table is in the middle of the room. I swear every pair of eyes in the place passes over me as I creep by. I feel the outraged glare in some of them.

Outrage or no, in less than a minute I'm easing the heavy door closed behind me. Free! I gaze the length of the hall. Now what? The pool? No chance. The games room? There's a fitness room too. Ha! There are books in my suitcase. And homework. And TV, of course. In the room, not the suitcase.

Kaya would go swimming. And maybe to the games room.

I wander in the general direction of our room, but the idea of being shut up in there by myself hurts. It actually hurts. In my head and my gut. In the end, I have no choice. Alone it is. Back in the room, I turn on the TV loud and find an old comedy from before I was born.

When I wake up in the middle of the night, the covers are over me, and the light and the TV have been turned off. I didn't even hear Mom come in. I roll over and toss and turn for the rest of the night, still in my clothes, listening to Mom snore.

The next day passes as slowly as that first night, except that now I'm tired and extra grumpy. No matter what I do, I can't stop thinking about Kaya, imagining her arriving at the house and finding it locked, realizing that her mother and her sister have abandoned her.

She'll get in somehow, I realize at one point. And I smile. She will. We'll get home to find a window at the back of the house broken and Kaya lounging in front of the TV. I feel a bit better after that.

Better, but still bored.

I actually squeeze myself into my swimsuit and swim six

lengths of the tiny pool, ready to leap out of the water and escape at the first sign of another human. After, I skip the shower and blow my chlorine-soaked hair into a frizzy cloud with the minuscule blow-dryer back in the room.

I go to the games room and try an old-fashioned pinball machine where every ball has a death wish. And finally I do what I really wanted to do all along. I buy a bottle of Coke and a bag of red Twizzlers and read and eat and drink for half an hour in bed. And it still isn't even time for lunch.

In the afternoon, I concentrate on sleeping and hating my mother. Every time Kaya tries to get into my head, I toss her out.

At last the time comes for another dinner. Between naps I've been conjuring that dessert table in my mind. Maybe I'll try the cheesecake tonight. With strawberry sauce. Maybe I'll walk right out of there with my dessert in hand, so's not to abandon half of it when the speaker starts. Either that or I'll eat even faster than usual.

I'm working my way through my lasagna at a satisfactory pace when a young man on the other side of Mom speaks. I take another bite, and jump when Mom elbows me in the side.

"Ron is speaking to you," she says sharply.

I swallow, raise my eyes and set my brain on playback. "So, a magician!" he has just said. "I think they had you in mind, young lady, when they booked tonight's entertainment!"

I try to smile as I dig my fork into the next bite. A magician? Magicians are for little kids' birthday parties. How old does he think I am?

Mom rescues me. "I'm exhausted," she's saying, "and tomorrow will be a long day with the drive home. I think I'm going to take a bath and read my book in bed."

Lasagna gone, I head for the dessert table, which is awash in puddings tonight. Even better than cakes! I heap my plate with trifle, bread pudding and a small scoop of chocolate mousse. Back at the table, Mom eyes my choices.

"Are you sure you want all that, honey?"

I look up and catch that man, Ron, looking at me. Is that pity on his face? Humiliation licks at my lower back. I take a bite and let my teeth sink through the sweet, creamy bread. Perfect. I angle myself away from my judgmental mother and the sympathetic man and take another bite. Trifle this time.

Mom has taken a pretty healthy serving of dessert herself. She cleans her plate, gulps down a coffee, says good night to everyone at the table and pushes herself to her feet. "Are you all set, Beth?" she says.

I look up at her.

"You should stay," the man says, "and watch the magician. He's supposed to be very good."

"Okay," I say, surprising myself and Mom both.

Δ

It's pretty embarrassing at first. The guy is in his fifties, probably, dressed in a tux with a red rose in the buttonhole, skinny, with longish grey hair and a longer-than-longish moustache. He plays to the crowd and the crowd is mostly women almost as old as he is. He picks out a jovial older man to be his assistant and the butt of his jokes, which are pretty rude, some of them. My table is near the front, and at first I'm afraid that he'll set eyes on me and try to draw me in somehow.

Then I get interested. He does stuff that doesn't seem all that original, stuff with ropes, for instance—he even pulls a toy rabbit out of a hat—but I watch closely, looking for the tricks, sure that from so close I will be able to see them. And I can't. Not once. I start to worry that the act is going to end.

He asks the man for a twenty-dollar bill, which the man hands over reluctantly. Hamming it up. The magician has chosen his assistant well. He tears a corner off the bill and asks the man to look at the two pieces and confirm that both have the same serial number. The magician leaves the larger portion of the bill with the man and tucks the tiny bit away. The trick continues, growing more and more complicated, until the magician pulls a lemon out of his pocket. The man examines the lemon and confirms it's whole. "This lemon has not been tampered with," he says, holding the lemon high in the air. Giggles ripple through the audience.

The magician takes a sharp knife and cuts into the lemon all the way round. He cuts a little deeper. Then he asks the man to hold one end while he holds the other. Together, they wiggle the lemon apart. The audience—and the man—gasp. Nestled in the heart of the lemon is a tightly rolled bit of paper, which turns out to be a quarter of a twenty-dollar bill with the same serial number as the one that the man handed over earlier.

The lemon trick is the magician's grand finale, and after that people begin to go back to their rooms, but some stay and chat a bit, several gathered around the magician, asking him questions and thanking him. I edge closer, listening. He isn't going to share his secrets, of course. I know better than that. But a question is nagging at me. I listen, hoping someone else will ask. Hoping I'll find out what I need to know without speaking to the magician myself.

But nobody does.

A voice in my ear makes me jump. "Glad you stayed?" the man asks, the same one who told me I should.

I positively beam at him as I nod.

"Interested in magic?" he asks.

Further nodding seems excessive. "Yes," I say instead.

He leaves then, and soon the two stragglers leave as well and the magician begins gathering up his things. My chance is slipping away.

I breathe in courage, breathe out words: "How did you get involved in magic?"

He jumps, just like I did moments earlier, jumps and turns. "Oh, I didn't see you there!" he says. "You startled me." He shows no sign that he has heard my question.

I almost turn tail, as they say. But with his eyes on my face, I find myself drawing breath once again, and asking the question a second time.

His eyes turn away from me then, and I can see him plunging into his memories. "My uncle taught me a couple of tricks when I was a kid and I never looked back," he says.

I stare at him. My eyes fix on his as my own memory overwhelms me: Mr. Duncan, Grade Four. I manage a smile. "Thank you, Mr. Jackson. I loved your show!"

And off I go to sneak into bed without waking Mom. I have a lot of thinking to do.

CHAPTER SIX

Beth

My memories lead me back and back, past Mr. Duncan and the magic tricks, all the way to the start of Grade Four, when I first realized something was wrong. That was two whole years after Dad was diagnosed. Before that, I just thought he went for treatments for some sickness, like when I got the flu or something.

I waited for him to get better. I asked him to play games with me or listen to me read as I learned how. He hardly ever said yes. And when he did let me read to him, he didn't really listen. He sat in his big chair with his eyes closed. If I stopped to test him, his eyes would open after a few seconds and he would look over at me, and I would carry on. When I stopped altogether, he would nod and smile and say thank you. But he never commented on what I was reading or asked me questions about it. And Mom just never had time for it at all.

Δ

No one mentioned the word *cancer*. Not until a girl I hardly knew sidled up to me at school one day.

"I'm really sorry about your dad," she said, stretching the word *dad* out long and sad.

I almost didn't answer. I almost walked away. A cloud of dread rose inside me.

"Sorry why?" I said, even though I did not, *did not*, want to know the answer.

The girl's eyes widened. "I don't know. I guess I made a mistake . . ."

I watched her gather momentum for flight, and was surprised by what my arm did then, shooting out and grabbing the girl's wrist, hard. She gave a loud squawk.

"Sorry *why*?" I said again.

"Let go of me."

I let go. "Tell me," I said.

The girl scrubbed at her bruised wrist and raised large, damp eyes to my face. Her lips quivered. "Cancer," she said. She rubbed at her arm some more. "My mom says your dad's going to die."

Up until then, I wasn't a bad student. I wasn't brilliant, that's for sure, but I wasn't bad. After the girl spoke the *C* word, school changed.

At home, Dad seemed all right. Things went on the same, more or less, for the rest of the year.

But at school, the other kids just kind of drifted away. I saw them whispering about me; I felt their soft drifts of pity. When they came close, I saw the fear in their eyes and felt my own fear unfurl and send tendrils up my spine and into my brain, along my veins and into my heart. School became the place where my dad was dying.

Δ

In January, the new teacher came: Mr. Duncan. He was new to the school, not just to our class, so he didn't know about my dad. Or so I thought at the time. He smiled at me, and his smile was bright and kind. His expectations were high. When he found out that I still had not mastered parts of Grade Three math, he sat down with me to work out how I would get caught up.

Hope stirred in my heart. Maybe Dad wasn't dying after all.

Then Mr. Duncan did the magic trick. It was a simple one, really. With cards. You had to take a card from the pack, and Mr. Duncan told you which card you had pulled. Every single time. The whole class surrounded him as he did it, watching from every angle. They examined the cards over and over again. They quizzed him mercilessly. But Mr. Duncan just smiled that bright smile and put the cards away until next time.

I had seen magic tricks on TV, but I had never seen anyone do one for real.

After the first time, I lay awake in bed, running through it in my mind: the teacher splaying out the cards, Ben hesitating and finally sliding one out, looking at it and holding it face down against his chest, the teacher putting the cards down in a stack and asking someone to cut the deck. After that, it was hard to get the steps quite right, except for the last one, the one where Mr. Duncan said, the first time, "Is it the nine of hearts?" and Ben's whole body gathered itself into a whoop of joy. "It is!" he said, flourishing the card so that the whole class could see.

And it was.

I knew it was just a trick. But it seemed like something else. It seemed like the magic of Narnia or Middle Earth. It seemed like Mr. Duncan had special powers. I dug an old deck of cards out of the games cupboard and set myself to learning how to shuffle.

Kaya hovered. "Can I try?" she begged.

"Your hands are too small," I said. "You'd just drop them."

Kaya stuck around long enough to watch me drop the cards myself, not once but three times.

"My hands aren't that small," she said at last.

I was about to tell her to find her own deck of cards, when the doorbell rang. It was Kaya's friend Diana, collecting her to play in the ravine. Off they went.

"Beth, why don't you go too?" Mom called from the kitchen.

Why would I hang out with a couple of little kids? Besides, I had work to do.

Δ

I should have been studying fractions instead of trying to master the art of the shuffle. I was going to be tested on Tuesday, my very own private test.

On Monday morning, Mr. Duncan stopped by my desk. "Have I got a deal for you!" he said jauntily.

I glanced around the room, but various projects were underway and no one seemed to be listening in. I managed a small smile. And waited.

"You have an important math test tomorrow," Mr. Duncan said. "I'm going to set you up back there to do it." He gestured toward a small round table under the window. "And I'd like to offer you a reward."

I was curious now.

"If you pass the test, you will join the rest of the class in the Grade Four book." He paused. I already knew about that. Mr. Duncan was leading up to something else. I guessed that if he had a drum set handy, he would ask for a drum roll, or perhaps he would beat one out himself. "If you pass the test, I will teach you the card trick I did last week."

"Really?" I said. "Do you . . . do you think I could do it?"

"Of course you can, Beth. The question is, Can you pass the math test? I believe that you can. That's why I'm making you this very special offer." He smiled again, but there was a challenge in it this time. A *show me what you're made of* kind of challenge.

I pulled the Grade Three math book out of my desk. Shuffling would have to wait.

Δ

The test the next day was tough. I spent an hour at that back table, working my way through two whole pages of questions, using up sheet after sheet of scrap paper, trying to show my work and get the right answers. Getting the right answer didn't matter much to Mr. Duncan if you didn't show the steps, and they couldn't just be scribbles either.

When I was done I looked over my work and shrank a little inside. It was smudged and scrinchy with lots scratched out. Oh well. It was over now. I put the messy pages into Mr. Duncan's hands. He announced a free period and settled down to mark the test right then and there while the class erupted in excitement and organized itself into groups for games. I got my cards out of my desk and cut the deck in two. I hadn't learned to do that flippy thing yet, where you divided and shuffled all in one long, smooth motion, but the shuffling itself was going pretty well. Not so many chunks of cards now.

I didn't really notice that any time had gone by when Mr. Duncan pulled a chair up beside my desk. "You did it," he said. "You got eleven out of twenty right. And you showed all your work!"

I looked at the paper Mr. Duncan had placed in front of me. So many Xs down the side of the paper, even though they were small. Mr. Duncan made his checks bigger than his Xs, but that didn't make the wrong answers right. His hand lighted on my shoulder.

"You got five out of twenty on the last one, if you remember," he said. "You figured out more than twice as many this time! I'll meet you here after lunch when everyone's outside, and we'll do some magic."

I sat perfectly still for a long moment after he stood up and told the class to return to their desks. I was caught in the glow of that light touch, those kind words, the anticipation of the session at lunch, and of what I would learn.

△

When I got home that day, Dad was in the den as usual; I could see him from the front hall. He didn't turn his head. He never did. He never seemed to hear me enter over the TV, which filled the room with sound and glare all day and all night. I usually walked on by, into the kitchen looking for a snack. Today, though, I went and stood in the doorway.

He had a magazine open in his lap and he did not look up. On the TV, someone was talking on the deck of an enormous ship.

I took another step into the room. "Dad," I said. "Dad."

He heard me the second time.

I pulled the battered cards out of my pocket.

"Pick a card, any card." I smiled as I said it, or tried to.

He smiled too, but his smile looked as stiff as mine felt. "What's this?" he said.

"A trick," I replied as I fanned the cards out in front of him. "Pick a card."

His smile grew. His eyebrows crinkled together. He reached for the remote and silenced the man on the deck of that ship. "Don't I get to cut the deck first?" he said.

My next breath filled my lungs right up, and I realized that I hadn't been breathing. I let him cut the deck; I fanned the cards. He picked one. And my story sprang out of me then, long and joyous: the trick, the deal, the test, the eleven check marks down the side of the page, the Grade Four math book, the magic lesson. While I talked, I was reviewing the next steps of the trick in my mind. The story, I realized, was the perfect distraction, and distraction was the key.

"Are you holding the jack of clubs?" I said at last, tying the question to the story, making it the grand finale.

He was.

Kaya slipped into the room not long after that, and Mom followed soon after to find the three of us sharing milk and cookies. I watched my mother look for something wrong with the scene, and I saw her tiny huff of acceptance when she realized that Dad was fine. Better than fine.

Then, "Show them, Beth," Dad said.

"I've got groceries to put away," Mom said.

"Come on, Margaret. Five minutes."

I flinched. I hated those exchanges between Mom and Dad, all sharp edges.

"Yes, show us!" Kaya said, spraying bits of cookie as she spoke.

And I did. I let Kaya pick the card. I prattled on a bit about how I had learned the trick, but I was nervous now, and it didn't come out right. I tried to follow the steps as I talked, but in the end I knew I was guessing when I said, "Is it the six of clubs?"

Kaya's face got sad, and my stomach turned over as I looked at the card face up in Kaya's hand: the queen of hearts.

"Hmm," Mom said. "More practice, I guess." She was heading for the kitchen as she said it.

"You'll get it, Beth," Dad said quietly, tipping Kaya off his lap. "You only just learned it today." He reached for the remote.

I shoved the cards into my pocket and went to my room, followed by my little sister. "Show me again," Kaya said. "I'll bet it works this time."

"No," I said shortly. "I've got homework."

Δ

It wasn't just the cards that showed up the holes in my life. The other kids shying away from me at school, Dad buried in his big chair, Mom, her whole body so tense she could have been made of stone, Kaya with her sad, crumpled face. It seemed as if Dad's cancer swirled everyone off somewhere far, far away, leaving me alone at the centre of a vortex.

For an hour or two I had thought that the magic would close the gap. But soon, off they went, swirling away again. I was discouraged, but I still hoped. I still imagined. In fact, I loved the cards, even though I couldn't make the trick work more than that one time.

Two weeks later, Mr. Duncan did another trick for the class. And the next day, he offered me another deal, science this time. I knew by then that Mr. Duncan was singling me out because of Dad. Or I was pretty sure. I didn't like that idea much, but I did want to learn the new trick. I had practised the first one quite a bit since the failed attempt with Mom and Kaya, but it was hard to work the kinks out all alone, with no one to try the trick out on.

I passed the test and learned the trick (sort of), but it turned out that Mr. Duncan only knew two. There wouldn't be a third. And the second trick was a lot harder than the first. I didn't have the guts to try it out on anyone, not even Dad.

Slowly, hope faded. What was a magic trick or two in the face of the *C* word anyway? I put the cards away in a drawer, and didn't shuffle another deck for a long, long time.

Δ

Dad lived for another five years, and the gaps and the hollows in our household grew and grew, even though he was in remission for a big part of that and he went back to work and everything.

He got sick again just as I started Grade Eight. Right around then, the girl who had told me about Dad's cancer in Grade Four marched up to me one day in the hall. Another girl was behind her, almost shadowing her.

"My mom says your dad's sick again," Jane said. I knew her name by then, of course. We'd been in school together for four years. "Want to sit with us at lunch?"

"I'm Samantha," the other girl said.

Samantha was new to the school and Jane had taken her on, like a pet. I was pet number two, I guess, a poor downtrodden creature who'd been rotting away all alone at the Humane Society.

I looked at them and considered Jane's question. I couldn't see any reason to say no.

"Sure," I said.

That's how I got to have friends.

I didn't like Jane's bossy ways, and often wished Samantha would stand up for herself, but it was kind of nice to have people to eat lunch with, and hang out with sometimes after school. Jane was always asking how Dad was doing. I didn't tell her much, even though he did worse and worse all through Grade Eight. He died at the start of Grade Nine.

Δ

Within days of Dad's death, Mom brought home a great big gangly collie puppy that she had bought all on her own without saying a word to Kaya or me first. Kaya fell in love with Sybilla instantly. They were always all wrapped up together on the couch or in her room. I couldn't help feeling hurt that Mom went off and bought that dog all by herself, and that Sybilla loved Kaya so very, very much.

Another day, perhaps a month after Sybilla came home, I was on my way down the stairs, all dopey from a nap, when Mom and Kaya came in the front door. Kaya was alight in a way that I hadn't seen for a long, long time. A kitten. She had a kitten in her arms. Behind her, Mom grinned.

I took a step forward, stopped and swayed, almost weak-kneed. Jealousy snaked through my legs and my skull and met and tangled in my chest. First a dog, now a kitten.

"Kaya came with me to get groceries and look what we got instead!" Mom said.

Δ

Now, at the lodge, I dream of magic tricks and dying fathers, with Sybilla and Coco, Jane and Samantha, thrown in.

Δ

On Sunday morning, Mom heads off to her last workshop and I make my way to the lodge's gift shop in search of a deck of cards. Back in our room, with our bags sitting side by side on the bed, I pull out the chair at the small round table under the window and set down the brand new deck precisely in the middle of the black surface. I look at it and breathe.

Excitement burbles inside me, small, like the tiniest brook, enticing. I pick the deck up again—it's red with one of those patterns that serious cards have, no pretty paintings or lush landscapes, just simple geometry in red and white—and run my fingers over the smooth cellophane, find the thin blue line that encircles the deck. I take the tiny tab between my thumb and forefinger, and pull. In one smooth motion, the clear wrapping comes away from the top of the box. I have only to slide the bottom part off, and I'm in.

The cards are slick in my hands, and after my first attempt at a shuffle I have to scrabble on the carpet to salvage a fallen queen and a three and a seven. They are beautiful, though, and, slippery though they may be, I love them, every one. I try another shuffle. And another. I start up a patter in the empty room, engaging an imaginary audience, and slide a card out of the deck, almost convincing myself that my own hand is someone else's.

For a moment I wish I had a subject, an audience, but it's too soon. Way too soon. Still, the morning passes in a flash. I almost forget to watch the clock. But not quite. When Mom comes back from her session just before noon, I'm sitting on my unmade bed, reading *Sandry's Book*, cards tucked out of sight.

CHAPTER SEVEN

Beth

Apparently Mom's morning was not as much fun as mine. She's clutching a fistful of pamphlets and business cards; her shoulders are slouched, her face dark. "Let's go," she says, hefting her bag over her shoulder. "We've got a long drive."

In the car she doesn't say much, and I'm pretty much oblivious to her misery, or I try to be, playing out in my mind the two card tricks I know, fingers caressing the deck in my pocket.

"Abuse, abuse, abuse," Mom says at one point, and the harsh word wrenches me to attention. "It's all they talk about with runaways."

She isn't talking to me. And she doesn't say anything else for a while. I sit there, magic tricks forgotten, as prickles run down my arms and into my fingers. Mom is chewing on her lower lip and staring so intently at the highway, it's a wonder her eyes don't pop out of their sockets.

I know we're both thinking and wondering the same things. Dad died. Yes. Our family was kind of messed up by it. But would Kaya run away because of that? Why?

Mom glances over at me sitting stiffly in my seat. "Are you all right, sweetheart?" she says.

Normally, I could be hanging out the car door ready to throw myself into the canyon before she would take notice.

"Oh, nothing," I say. "I think I'm just tired."

Mom huffs and is quiet again. After a bit, "Kaya's the exception to the rule," she says. "I wish they wouldn't generalize like that, as if kids are all the same."

Then she starts in about homework. The moment passes, but not the word that has brought it about. I have only to let my mind brush up against it—*abuse*—and there are those prickles, all over again.

Mom goes silent again once we pass Hope. Magic tricks and questions about the past fade from my mind as we enter the heavy back-to-the-city-on-Sunday-afternoon traffic. My thoughts turn to my sister right now, today. I'm sure Mom is thinking about Kaya too.

Will the house be empty? And if it is empty, which kind of empty? Empty ever-since-Friday, or empty someone-came-and-went-on-Saturday? I can't quite bring myself to hope that Kaya will actually be there. I'm not sure I want to set eyes on her right now.

It starts to rain as we approach the bridge, and traffic slows to a crawl. Mom's fingers tap the steering wheel. I turn up the volume on my Walkman and try not to grit my teeth. I finger the cards in my pocket again, but it does no good at all.

Δ

As soon as I walk through the front door, I see the light blinking like crazy on the phone. Messages.

Mom is behind me, unloading the car.

"Just put that down and come back and help," she shouts, but I ignore her.

The dash to get the receiver into my hand is instinctive, but once I'm holding it, I freeze. It will be about Kaya. I know that. But what? Who?

The front door bangs against the wall as Mom comes through laden and angry. "Couldn't you do what I—?"

She sees the phone in my hand and stops speaking, her eyes fixed on the blinking light. In a moment her bags are on the ground and she is at my side, holding out her hand.

"I checked for messages just this morning," she mumbles.

She's brisk as she pushes the buttons, and her face is businesslike as she listens. She presses the "off" button and looks at me.

"Well, she's not dead," she says, "or hurt." She pauses. "Apparently, she's in jail."

"Jail?" I say blankly. "But she's . . ."

"All right, the youth detention centre."

It isn't quite that something has happened *to* Kaya, as it turns out. Kaya has done something to someone else. And now she's in custody. And they're going to hold her overnight. At least.

"Get your coat, Beth. We're going to see her. Oh, and could you get her toothbrush and some clean clothes from upstairs?"

I stare at Mom. "Where are we going? Where is this place?" I hear my voice rising as I speak, but I can't help it.

Mom's face tenses. She breathes, tries to calm herself, but it doesn't work.

"Burnaby," she says. "Willingdon Youth Detention Centre, it's called. Now will you go fetch her things?"

I don't know how I can go from scared to angry so fast, but I do.

"So Kaya punches someone, and now I have to visit her in some kind of jail?"

Mom's whole face contracts. "Yes," she says. "That's precisely correct. If you can't get her things, go wait in the car. I'll get them."

"I'm doing it," I say. Angry. Angry. Angry. "I can't believe this."

Upstairs, I shove a toothbrush in a bag and root around in Kaya's nightmare bedroom for pants and a shirt. Won't she be wearing striped pyjamas anyway?

On the way out, I grab my own bag, with my Walkman, my book and the leftover jelly beans from the Chilliwack gas station. I shove those deep in my coat pocket. Mom has already started the car by the time I get there.

We drive most of the way in silence.

"Be kind," Mom says as we wind our way up to the youth detention centre.

I stare out the window at the high wire fences that keep the world safe from kids like my sister. *Kind.* I let my teeth sink through the jelly bean in my mouth and swallow the two resulting lumps of gelatin, feeling them all the way down my throat. Then I wrestle another candy out of my pocket and sneak it into my mouth. *Kind.* I will be kind.

I sit alone in a waiting room while Mom meets with some people. Despite my best efforts I feel two tears escape, one from each eye. I slip yet another jelly bean into my mouth and swipe at my eyes. Then we both have to put all our possessions, jelly beans included, in a locker. A guard upends the bag that I threw together and rifles through it with gloved hands.

"She won't need any of this," she says shortly. "We supply toiletries and clothes."

Mom looks sad as she takes the bag from the guard and stows it in the locker along with everything else. "Can we see her now?" she asks.

"This way, please," the guard says.

She leads us to a metal detector, but Mom stops halfway, her hands flying to her face. "I should have brought her a book. Or something to eat."

I stand and watch Mom cry. The guard watches too. My hand rises from my side just a little, as if I were thinking of resting it on Mom's heaving back, but some powerful force holds us apart. My arm falls back.

"I have some jelly beans," I say at last. "We could give her those."

The guard nods and turns back toward the lockers. "You could," she says, "if you like."

I think about *Sandry's Book*, tucked away in my bag. I'm halfway through, loving it, and it's part of a series. I press my lips together as I reach into the bottom of the locker and slide the slightly sticky, half-empty bag of candy from my jacket pocket. I leave my bag alone, book safely stored for later on, when I am safe at home in my own bed. I am not giving up that book.

Mom has managed to stop crying, and the negative force field between us doesn't seem to affect her, because she yanks me to her in a quick hug. "You're a sweetheart," she says with a loud sniffle.

I square my shoulders as I walk through the metal detector. Mom's hug drops off me like water off butter.

And there is Kaya, sitting on a couch alone, eyes on us as we enter the room. "Sweetheart," Mom practically shouts, and I flinch.

"I'll be right here," the guard says. "You have half an hour."

Δ

Kaya speaks fast, so fast that I only understand about two-thirds. Her tone is angry and self-righteous. The other girl deserved it. She'd been making everyone miserable for a long, long time. One of the girls was going to talk to her pimp, and that would have been the end of it.

Pimp. I see Mom's back tense. Myself, I push the word away. I'll think about it another time, not here, while I listen to my baby sister rattle on about her crimes. In a *jail*.

"So I taught her a lesson." She grins. "I never punched someone before, you know? But she went down. And I said, 'Listen. You got to stop this stuff, else you're really going to get hurt.' And those red-cap guys were right there. A guy and a girl. They heard me threaten her. That's what they said when they were arresting me. A citizen's arrest . . . What bullshit! I didn't threaten her. I warned her. I was helping her."

My mouth opens. I hear the sarcasm packed around my words, but I can't seem to do anything about it. "I see. You *helped* her by punching her in the face."

Kaya's eyes have been fixed on Mom's face until now. She glances at me, but turns right back to Mom. "Beth's just like them. She doesn't get it." She pauses. "I didn't totally mean to punch her in the face."

Mom has been nodding throughout Kaya's speech, one hand on Kaya's knee. Now she speaks. "Well, Kaya. We just want you home. And if you go around attacking people, you're not going to get to come home. It's not safe for you . . ."

I watch Kaya's eyes drop as she takes in what Mom is saying.

"Mom," I say, "she shouldn't punch people, because it's wrong. She deserved to be arrested."

Mom reaches behind her with a silencing hand. "Shush, Beth. We're here to support your sister."

In the same moment, Kaya's eyes come back up, filled now with betrayal. "Guard," she says, "I want to go."

"Kaya," Mom says, her voice breaking on the word, becoming a wail.

It ends then, the visit. On the way out, I shove my hand in my pocket and find the jelly beans, stickier now, but still mine.

Δ

The drive home is awful. Mom cries for half the journey and yells at me the other half. I clench my teeth. Curl my fists. Tighten every muscle in my body. But despite my best efforts, those high fences creep back into my mind, along with an image of my little sister huddled all alone on that couch, staring at us with eyes that seem hungry now, though they seemed fierce then.

As I replay Kaya's frenzied speech, the bravado is obvious. *I didn't totally mean to punch her in the face.*

Kaya's misery floods through me; I can't keep it away. I tip my head against the car window and shrink at the thought of her alone in a cell, or worse, crammed into one with girls who happily punch others in the face, or stick knives in their guts if they smile wrong.

Home. I use my jelly beans and my book to soothe myself. It works nicely until I remember that Kaya is supposed to be enjoying the candy right now.

The night that follows is long.

Kaya

You tell them you were teaching her a lesson, but really it wasn't like that at all. It all just kind of happened. The other girl was so frustrating. Amber, her name was. She was young, though not as young as you. Skinny, but pretty, with a really round face and huge eyes. And she just showed up one day, kind of muscled in on things.

One of the pimped girls, Gemini, was furious when she found Amber standing on her corner. "Waggling her hips like a crazy person" was how Gemini put it.

You'd had a chance to talk to Amber earlier, heard a bit of her story. She came from Calgary; she'd been on the street there a little bit. She couldn't go home 'cause her dad beat her up. Then they stuck her in a group home and that was it for her. She'd heard Vancouver was a good place to be.

"If this doesn't work out for me, there's always Victoria," she said, grinning.

She had to be scared, but she didn't show it, and you admired that. You liked her, really. But she had not one single clue. When Gemini found Amber on her corner, she was ready to go straight to her pimp, which wasn't fair.

"Why don't you talk to her?" you said to Gemini. "You talked to me."

"You were ready to listen," she said.

"And she isn't?"

"She'll listen to him."

It made you sick to your stomach when she said that. You remembered Jim's weight on you in that filthy bed, the way he just expected that, like you owed it to him or something. He'd never hit you, but you'd seen other girls with big hand-shaped bruises on their arms.

Just last week, a girl had her head shaved by this same guy Gemini was talking about. The story went round, putting fear into all of them, and you saw the girl, or you were pretty sure you did. She was running with a scarf kind of falling off her head, and you saw a flash of bare scalp, with a big bloody patch. They didn't shave gently. You were lucky to have escaped it yourself, you knew. And Gemini would give someone over to that?

"I gotta go," you said.

And ten minutes later, you were being arrested by a couple of do-gooders in red caps, while Amber pulled herself to a sitting position and held her jaw. "You punched me," she said slowly.

They wouldn't even let you answer.

Well, in a way she did deserve it. And maybe it would make her pay attention. She sure hadn't listened before. "I'll work where I want," she'd said. "You can't own a corner!" You took hold of her arm to pull her away from there, and she wrenched herself free, and when you reached out again, she shoved you, and next thing you knew, your fist was connecting with her face.

Δ

Fourteen days have already passed.

They don't call it jail, but it might as well be. When you stood up in the courtroom and heard the judge say *ninety days*, your knees actually went weak. Mom was crying in the background, but you didn't look at her. Beth was at school, apparently.

And fourteen nasty days they have been. Withdrawal hit you hard, and the folks sure don't ease you through it here, though you've heard there are ways to do that. Endless fits of puking, mostly bile, liquid shit, whole body burning and freezing, aching joints. Sometimes all at the same time. You would have given anything for a fix. Or death. You didn't really care which. You got through it, though.

Back when you got here, they offered to let you go home until court, but Mom looked really nervous when they said that, and you just said, "Hey. No. I'll stay here, thanks." Anyway, it's a good thing, because you can't imagine withdrawing at home with Mom and Beth.

The first dozen or so of your remaining seventy-six days pass, one by one. And you settle down after a bit. At first, it's hard not to mouth people off because it's all so ridiculous, and there are those high fences, and you were only trying to help that girl.

Then, sometime in early June, you get practical.

Δ

It happens during one of Mom's visits, after she mentions Hornby.

You think back and back, all the way to the Hornby trip when you were still a little kid, five or six. Dad was alive. He wasn't even sick yet, or if he was, you didn't know it. You camped, right near Big Tribune, the best beach in the whole entire world.

Every single morning of that holiday, you all walked from the campsite along the beach, lugging your supplies for the day, found the very best spot and set yourselves up, constructing a shelter out of one big beach umbrella and all the weathered wood you could drag into place.

In the afternoon, you and Beth would watch for the ice cream guy. "Ice cream!" you shrieked together when you saw him, and Dad would give you a stack of quarters, enough for an ice cream cone each. Sometimes he would come along and get cones for himself and Mom too. You and Dad always had chocolate. Beth had strawberry. And Mom had vanilla.

"Together we're Neapolitan," Mom said once, and you all laughed.

Dad taught you to swim that summer, and you took to

the water right off even though you were just five, loving it just like Dad did. Mom and Beth would walk to the pebble cove while you cavorted in the shallows.

They always went on and on about it after: how they would turn over rocks and watch the scurrying crabs, poke at geoduck holes and jump back, shrieking, when the water squirted up past Beth's waist. And how they looked for glass. Beth still has the pieces she found that summer.

Sometimes you wanted to go with them on those long walks, but the water was better than crabs and geoducks and bits of glass. The water was your home.

But that was before, you think, your insides constricting, because now you remember last year. That guy, Adam, in the car.

How many other men have there been since then? Men who looked at you with disgust; men who paid you and then turned you out of their cars. Can Hornby possibly feel the same after all that? If it could . . . The longing you feel as you ponder that question is so deep that you have to put your hands on your knees and breathe for long seconds, while Mom looks at you, brows pulled together, lips sealed.

When you meet her eyes again, her face clears. All practicality, she says, "You're supposed to get out on August ninth, but they told me that you can get out early, a whole week early, if you work hard. We'll pick you up here and drive straight to the ferry."

That gets your attention. Anything to get away from the city.

"You're a changed woman," one of the guards says a few days later as she unlocks the door between the classrooms and the refectory. And she only has a slight edge to her voice as she says it.

And you are, at least on the outside. It's the notebook that makes it possible. A social worker gave it to you early in your stay, along with one pen, but you don't start writing in it till after you know about Hornby. They keep a close watch on pens here; you have to trade one in to get another one, but at least they're allowed. Anyway, you draw a bit, but the lines on those notebook pages just beg for words. They're like greedy little puppies. You feed them and feed them, little stories and poems, taking moments from your time downtown and turning them into things between the covers of a book. You like it. Actually, you like it a lot.

On Monday, August third, you change into the clothes that Mom has dropped off for you, and wait with your tiny bag of possessions, your notebook safe in the bottom. Your stomach clenches and you actually have to go to the bathroom to retch for a minute or two. A year ago, Mom talked about a month on Hornby like it was the best cure in the world. Now, you all know it offers only a temporary escape. Still, it's better than this place, even though it means Mom and Beth for companions all day, every day, for four whole weeks.

CHAPTER EIGHT

Kaya

Summer is over. Hornby is behind you.

It wasn't so bad. You dozed and dove the days away on the beach, tanning a deep dark brown, and slipping into the water every time you got too hot. You avoided the hippie part of the beach, and stayed in at night, filling three sketch-books with pen-and-pencil drawings, and terrible, awful poems filled with agony and longing. They were a kind of angsty fun to write, as long as you didn't reread them afterward. You didn't even look in the prison notebook—that's what you call it to yourself—and you kept it well out of sight. Too hard to write anything real with Mom and Beth around all the time.

Mom tried to talk with you a few times, but eventually she gave up. Beth didn't even try. She practised card tricks endlessly from a stack of books on magic. She did ask to practise on you once, but quickly switched to Mom when you let her know what you thought of a sixteen-year-old girl pretending to be some kind of magician.

Now, summer is over. And you face home. School. All the people and places that breed dread in your belly.

Downtown is there too. Waiting.

On the first day of school, Mom has ordered Beth to wait for you, to bring you home from school in one piece. And Mom has ordered you to wait for your sister. You've decided to go along with them for a bit. See if you can stick it out. Grade Nine.

At three o'clock you tear yourself away from the fringe of the clutch of smokers at the edge of the trees. It's not as if they're speaking to you anyway. They ignore differently now. Instead of looking down their noses, they kind of skitter away. They know about the detention centre.

Michelle is here today too. She doesn't skitter.

She sucks on her cigarette like she'll die without it. You haven't seen each other in a long, long time.

"They put me in treatment," she says, and lets out a big smoky laugh. Treatment's a joke, apparently.

"I got arrested," you say. That's got to be one up, you think. And hate yourself.

She breathes out a cloud and sucks on her cigarette again. Smoke held in, she asks, "What did you do?"

"Punched a girl."

She breathes out and looks at you, hard. The rest of them are watching you, murmuring to each other. Drug addicts and delinquents. That's what you are.

No. That's what you *were*. You don't know about Michelle, but you're clean. You're clean and it's three o'clock, time to meet your sister out front and go home. Maybe you'll stay away from Michelle for a bit.

"I have to go," you say.

Michelle doesn't say a word. But it's hard to tear yourself away. Her eyes hold onto yours with a death grip.

For a long moment, you don't even try to free yourself. You look back, thinking hard. You avoided her all spring when you were going back and forth downtown. Gemini warned you off "girls like her," and the image of Michelle on that filthy bed made it easy to listen. The fact that you ended up nodding off in exactly the same spot with the same nasty man next to you just made you more determined to stay away from her.

You're done with downtown, with all of it. And that has got to include her, no matter how desperate she is.

Or precisely because of it.

Δ

Beth is sitting on the bottom step, with that awful pseudo-friend of hers, Jane, chattering away. Her other sort-of friend, Samantha, is hovering in the background looking kind. Jane sees you.

"How're you doing, Kaya?" she says. "I hear you spent some time in juvie atoning for your sins."

Nothing on earth could compel you to speak to Jane or even to look at her. "Let's go," you say to your sister.

Jane laughs.

She sounds like a braying donkey, you think, and suppress a small annoyed smile.

"Jane," Samantha says quietly, but Jane barely glances in her direction.

Beth hoists herself to her feet, and you feel your nose wrinkle at the sight of her. She sure has packed on the pounds over the summer. And she has such a big mouth, telling Jane about Willingdon. And Jane, it seems, has already told the whole school that you spent time in jail. Fury comes in a wave, and recedes. Disgust is easier anyway. Besides, you're staying home now. You can't afford to react. You can't.

Beth

Every minute of those first weeks of September is a pain. No. Every minute is *hell*.

First off, there's school.

I learn Kaya's schedule and keep checking up on her. At first I plan to do it just once or twice a day, but I can't help myself; it's like I'm spying on her, following her when I have a spare, and dropping in on her teachers during breaks and asking them if she's attending classes. Every afternoon, I wait out front, afraid that she's given me the slip, that she won't show, even though I always know that she's been in school all day. Most days, Jane manages to say something rude and Kaya lashes back, just as mean, and Samantha murmurs something or other. Kaya doesn't really show signs of running away, so maybe I should just relax and let her be, but I can't.

Then, there's Mom's job. She went and got herself a new one after we got back from that conference—she's less of a nurse now and more of a social worker, or some such thing—and she starts the same time we start school. So, she's trying to settle in at work, when as far as I'm concerned she should be making sure that Kaya settles in at home. She shuts herself in her room in the evenings, though how she can work in that mess, I don't know.

Every Saturday, she emerges for a few hours to have fun with Kaya, as if a movie or two will fix her. She does invite me along, but the plans are clearly hers and Kaya's. They go to *The Wedding Singer* one Saturday, *The Mask of Zorro* the next. They don't ask me what I want to see. Apparently surviving juvenile detention earns you the right to order up movies, meals and whatever else. I stay at home with the contents of the kitchen cupboards, which is sad since both those movies are supposed to be great. Yes, I know I'm sulking. No, I don't care.

Mom whispers at me once in a while about my weight, and Kaya makes snarky comments. I wear sweatpants and T-shirts and avoid mirrors, but I can feel the thickness when I move my arms or turn my head. Tomorrow I'll stop, I say. Tomorrow.

I practise my magic a lot, at least. I made leaps and bounds while we're on Hornby, and I'm still getting better every day, though I'm not ready to let anyone know. Samantha'd be all right, probably, but I can just imagine what Jane would say.

The magic soothes me—not just the doing of it, but the learning, the mastering. I think about that sometimes, about how good it feels, the deep concentration. I wonder about unravelling it from the soaps and the ice cream, which soothe me too. But I still get the best kick, the best flood of calm, when I've got all three going at the same time.

One afternoon when they're out at some matinee, I get

stuck on the box-to-box trick, making something appear somewhere else. I lose the thread of my muttered patter against the drone of the TV. I press the mute button, take another bite of ice cream and try again, but the boxes are all crooked and tippy on the bed.

Normally when this happens, I switch back to card tricks. I've rigged up a pretty good lap table with one of Mom's nursing books, and the cards stay put. Today, though, something's driving me. I have no idea what. I grab the remote, push the "off" button and shove the half-eaten Häagen-Dazs into the freezer, burying it under frozen peas and a couple of ancient steaks, white as snow.

It takes two minutes to clear the clutter off the dining table, to set up my boxes, long-eared rabbit at the ready. The blurry film in my head clears away, and my fingertips tingle as my brain tells my hands what to do. The patter flows, even though I'm only talking to myself. When I lift the second box at the end, there is the rabbit, gazing up at me through her beaded eyes, exactly where she is supposed to be, whisked there by my magic.

I drop onto a chair and burst into weird confusing tears.

Kaya

Every single day, you go to school, day after day, week after week. Well, for two weeks anyway. Almost every day, you see Diana, hanging out in the halls with her friends. When your eyes meet, though, she darts away.

The movies with Mom on the weekends are fun. Beth

is a big baby and won't come along, but it's nice being alone with Mom for a change. And you avoid the theatres downtown.

You can do this, you tell yourself. You can go to school like other kids, do your homework, learn a bit of math, some French. Hang out.

You pull out the prison notebook early on in those days at home, and fill up the last few pages on the rare occasions when you find yourself alone. When it's full, you hide it, and you hide it well.

You avoid Michelle for the whole first two weeks, but then you hear about a late-September beach party, and it sounds like fun. That's what normal kids do anyway, they don't go off to sleazy hotel rooms and shoot up: they party together. You can't face going alone, and Michelle's the closest thing you have to a friend, so you call her.

You climb out your window that night, after making sure that the sliding door is unlocked so you can get back in later. And Michelle is waiting on the corner, so you can hitchhike together. The bonfire's already huge when you get there, and lots of kids are wasted. Still, there are no needles here. No gross old men. You and Michelle hang out for a while, sharing a little bottle she stole from her foster parents. It feels so good, the liquor, warm in your belly and your chest. Nothing like the stuff you do downtown. This is what normal kids do. This is normal.

Michelle does get a bit out of hand, slurring and saying stuff you really, really don't want to hear. You stick with her, and the two of you head up the steps to Marine Drive fairly early, you supporting her a lot of the way. The guy who picks you up pretty much as soon as you stick out your thumb wants to take the two of you out to a club, but you just say no thanks, and he drops you off not too many blocks from home. He's even pretty nice about it.

Δ

Midway through that week, almost three whole weeks into the school year, you come out of a stall in the washroom to find Diana waiting for you. She doesn't just happen to be there. She's facing you, bracing herself on a sink. She looks awful.

You start to move past her toward the door, but she steps in front of you. "He's . . . he's dead," she says, finally.

That stills your flight. "What?" you say. "What?"

"He's dead," she says again, more wailing now than speaking. "He . . . he . . ."

"He what?" you say. Not *who*.

Diana's shoulders are shaking. She's actually sobbing. You wait for her, pondering the word *dead*. Can she really mean it? And, if so . . . "He . . . he shot himself," she says, the words drawn out through her sobs. "In his front garden. Yesterday."

You stare at her for another long moment, searching tentatively inside yourself as you do. You do not try to comfort her. You do not feel sad yourself. Sad? That's crazy. Crazy.

Her sobs die down at last, and she looks at you like she wants something. What?

Something burbles deep down inside; it gathers force in your gut like lava in a volcano. It starts its way up. Up. Up. It's already high in your chest when you recognize it for what it is. Rage. It's white-hot rage.

"What do I care?" you say then, and you see her eyes widen, her shoulders curl forward, almost reaching for one another. She takes a step back. "Why are you telling me?" You're almost spitting, struggling to stop from shouting. "Can't you mind your own fucking—"

That's when three girls tumble together through the washroom door. They stop in their tracks, staring.

"Ooh," one of them says. "Drama!"

Diana takes an enormous breath. You know you've hurt her. But the knowledge does nothing to quell your rage. And she's gone. Out the door. You're close behind, but you turn the other way down the hall. You hope never to set eyes on that meddling bitch again.

CHAPTER NINE

Kaya

Your next class is English, and you surprise yourself by going.

The second you sit down, the rage swirls away. Inside, you shrivel up, but outside, you straighten your shoulders and paste your best sneer onto your face.

You grip the sides of your chair and tense up in self-defence, but the horror of it all scratches and pokes at your skin from the inside out. It's here now, and it's not going to go away.

After school, late that afternoon, you leave the house quietly. You are empty-handed, no change in your pocket for the bus, no bag of stuff, not even one of your teeny-tiny purses slung over your shoulder. Mom is in the kitchen. She can't hear the door from there. For once in her life, Beth is out.

Your feet walk you along the sidewalk. You look down at them, wondering. You reach the corner and turn . . . right, away from the buses on Tenth Avenue. Stop at the curb. Your stomach turns all the way over, twisting your intestines into a taut rope. You look both ways and cross the street.

Trudge, trudge. Your gut pulses painfully. Two blocks and you've reached Fourteenth. Right again. Halfway down the block you grit your teeth and insist that your feet stop. You can see the house just ahead. It's been a year, almost, since you last set eyes on it.

Minutes pass as you stand there, looking at the small grey stucco house, at the bushes, so overgrown that the front windows are almost invisible, at the dried-out lawn, surrounded now with yellow police tape. Along the walkway from house to sidewalk, the roses thrive. One of them is still in bloom, and you can see two blossoms from where you stand, big and pink: Queens of Sweden.

You are frozen on the sidewalk. Your eyes stare at the house, but don't see, so at first you don't notice the shift in the curtain, the face that peers out. There's a moment outside of time, when that woman is looking at you, and you know it, but you don't. Then you blink. That is not a happy face. She looks as if she's shouting, but you can't hear her through the glass.

She disappears from the window and a moment later the front door opens, and she's out on the front step, shouting audibly now. You're turning, running, the sound of her voice burning into your brain.

"Stay off my sidewalk—" are the only words you take in.

You don't look back. You run and you run and you run all the way home.

Standing in your bedroom, on that September afternoon, with your back to the door, your breath heaving out of you and in, you wish you had your hands on Diana's throat. You would strangle her on the spot. And she would deserve it. She would. She would. She would.

You throw yourself on your bed, but that is not a good place to be.

"Kaya?" you hear from outside your door.

"Leave me alone!" you scream.

Then you have to jump up and run past your sister to the bathroom, where you collapse onto your knees and throw up. You flush the toilet and kneel there, your forehead against the cool porcelain.

The horror keeps growing in your gut, your chest, a live thing. You only know one way to quiet it.

Beth

I stand there at the top of the stairs for a bit. I hear the toilet flush and figure she threw up. She wouldn't run past me like that just because she had to pee.

She doesn't know I saw her running outside. I was walking the dog—her dog—about to turn the corner onto Twelfth, almost home, when she came tearing out of a side street. Fourteenth, I'm pretty sure. She was charging toward me, but she didn't see me. I don't think she saw a thing. Lucky she wasn't hit by a car crossing the street. Anyway, I got into the house ahead of her and was standing in the living room when she burst in and charged up the stairs.

Now, Kaya shoves past me into her room, Sybilla at her heels. At least she'll let the dog comfort her.

I go downstairs and pause at the front door, thinking for a moment more before I put my coat on and head outside, dog-less now, down to the corner, up Discovery, two blocks, turn right. I walk slowly down Fourteenth, see the police tape and pause in front of that house. I stare a bit, until a woman yanks the front door open and glares at me. Her hair is a mess. She's wearing an ancient man's robe. Her feet are bare.

"This is private property," she says.

I'm standing on the sidewalk, but, "Sorry," I say, and walk on, pondering.

Δ

"Did you hear that that old man up on Fourteenth with all the toy cars and things killed himself yesterday?" Mom's friend says. "Shot himself in the head. Outside in his front garden at eleven o'clock in the morning."

She stops talking, looks pleased with herself. It's not yet noon on Saturday—Mom's not thrilled to have a visitor.

"I don't think I knew him," Mom says, her brow all crinkly.

But at the mention of the toy cars, I have gone rigid. I remember something. Two things. About the house on Fourteenth and the man who lived there.

I consider saying, "But, Mom, you do know him. He came to Dad's funeral." But I don't.

Mom is frowning. "Think about the kids on that street," she says, "and his children, if he had any."

"Oh, they said he did. On the radio," the friend says.

"Grown sons. Grandchildren too, I'd say. He was an elderly man. Seventy-nine."

I am staring now at Kaya, who is home today and up already, down on the floor in the corner of the kitchen with Coco. Her hand has stopped moving on the cat's back and her chin is up, her gaze fixed on the kettle, just about to boil.

"Was somebody going to make hot chocolate," she says.

I turn toward the counter, eager, all of a sudden, to put a cup of hot chocolate into my little sister's hand.

Kaya

You keep still in the kitchen that morning, only your right hand moving, after the briefest of pauses, over and over again, along the cat's spine. Then, when the topic of conversation shifts, you release the cat and struggle to your feet. And it is a struggle. Your legs have filled with ice.

You stand in the shower until the water runs cold and you begin to shake from the chill instead of from your own sobs. The liquid sluicing down your body and into the drain could be that man's blood, and no amount of showering will rinse all of it away.

When you come out of the bathroom with a towel clutched over your chest and return to your room, Beth is sitting on your bed.

"Are you all right?" she says. She stops talking then, as if her brain is thinking, thinking. Her eyes show concern. And fear.

You stand before her, dripping, blood and brain matter still clinging to your skin. You feel your mouth open, the word *no* begins to form somewhere in your belly. The *N* makes a leap all the way up into your throat—but it can't get out your mouth.

With a sharp shake of your head, you growl, "Can't I have a little privacy? Get the hell out of my room!" The fury that sweeps through you is almost refreshing.

Reliably, Beth's chin wobbles. She shoves a clump of hair behind her ear as she stands, eyes on the ground. "I . . ." she says. "I . . ." She stumbles out of the room, her shoulders already heaving before she manages to get the door closed behind her.

Her absence flings you back upon yourself, and the fear that you saw in her face ricochets through you. You know what would feel even better than torturing Beth, but you are resisting that. You've resisted it all the way since yesterday.

You shimmy into a pair of jeans and pull a T-shirt over your head. It's time to go downstairs and put on a show, convince your mother and your sister that there is nothing wrong with you. Not a thing. Maybe you can convince yourself while you're at it.

"How do pork chops and lemon meringue pie sound?" Mom says as you glide into the kitchen, the picture of happiness.

"Yum!" you reply. "I'll make the crust. Where's Beth?"

"In her room," Mom says. "She seems really upset about that man's suicide." She looks puzzled. "You don't think she knew him, do you?"

You know damn well why Beth is upset, but you let her misery slide into oblivion along with all that blood and brain matter and what it means. Oblivion is a big place, but it's getting pretty full and gross—really, really gross—like an overused outhouse. Don't look down, you tell yourself silently. Your voice in your head is sharp and bossy, and you need that right now.

Beth

I am tired. Every bit of me is tired. I'm so tired that when I leave Kaya, I don't even try to fight back the tears. I cross the landing to my room and fall onto my bed. I feel like falling to the floor instead, praying to some sort of god out there that what I suspect—what I am starting to know—is not true. It can't be true.

I lie there while the tears drain out of me, and slip into a weird kind of sleep.

I struggle when hands shake me, and force my eyes open to Mom's worried face.

"Supper's almost ready, sweetheart. Are you all right?" Mom says, and I nod blearily and slide my legs out of bed.

I wash my face and go downstairs to the smell of baking. In the kitchen, Kaya is pulling a pie, heaped with golden meringue, from the oven. Mom rushes out the back door to check something on the barbecue.

I slide along the bench behind the kitchen table, and let them bustle. Kaya looks fine, happy even. Maybe I'm wrong. Maybe the roses at Dad's funeral didn't mean a thing.

Δ

I was twelve, I guess, or maybe just thirteen, when I escaped the house one Saturday afternoon and went for a walk. Rare for me. Anyway, I was close to Fourteenth when a kid-sized car occupied by a great big boy tore across my path and almost hurtled right into the street.

"Sorry!" the boy shouted, grinning like crazy. He didn't look sorry at all.

"That was awesome!" another boy called as he ran right into my path as well.

Behind them came an old man, smiling broadly. He hobbled a bit, balanced on a cane, but he looked kind of elegant in a jacket and tie and an old-fashioned hat.

The second boy looked at me and we recognized each other in the same moment. From school.

"Hey," he said.

"Hi," I replied, awkward, looking for the words that would free me to continue on my way.

The man reached us and held out his hand. "I'm Mr. Grimsby," he said. "I live right up there. In the house with all the roses. Would you like a ride?"

"No, no," I said. "No, but thanks, Mr. . . . ."

"Grimsby," he said again. "Well, drop by anytime. That's what Paul and Dave do."

Grimsby, I thought, as I walked on. Grimsby. On the way home I passed the house again. The boys and the man were gone, but the roses and the toy car still sitting out on the front walk identified it for me. The rose bushes were in full bloom, all pinks and reds, and a massive birch tree in the backyard hooded the house in green.

I wouldn't mind riding a little car like that, I thought.

Then I imagined my bulk squeezed into the tiny seat. I

could just hear Mr. Grimsby's "I'm sorry, dear. You're just a bit too big."

I glimpsed Paul and Dave at school the next day, out in the breezeway. I could go up to them, start a conversation. After all, we had a topic, ready to go.

But I did not.

Δ

The second Grimsby event, the one where the roses were orange, not pink or red, came later. I am not going to think about that one today.

Δ

I'm both reassured and chilled by Kaya's smiles, by her gushing about her pie, and, as always, I manage to turn my attention to the food.

The dinner is good and I wolf down two helpings. Pork chops, heaps of boiled potatoes with lots of butter, corn on the cob. Green beans. Then the pie. Mom chatters away about work and her words are soothing, filling all the empty spaces. Kaya smiles and nods and nibbles. I gaze at her now and again, looking for signs. I try to tell myself that the smiles, the comments and the nibbles mean that my instincts are wrong. Kaya is just fine.

Kaya stands up as soon as she has taken her last bite. Her smile is bright and wide, but by now I'm not at all convinced that it's real. "Anyone want to watch a movie?" she says.

Mom smiles back, as always. "Yes, let's!" she says. "The dishes can wait."

She chooses *Mary Poppins*, and we all watch together, munching on popcorn with tons of butter, even though we're all full of chops and pie, and singing along to all the songs. I look over at Kaya at the end, when Mary Poppins is floating away over the London housetops, and tears are pouring down her face. The front of her T-shirt is wet.

She's been snuggled up to Mom through half the movie, and at the end, she kisses her on the cheek and gets up. "Good night, Mom," she says. Then, "Good night, Beth."

I don't like it that she says good night to me like that. I don't like it at all.

"Good night, Kaya," I say, but it feels more like goodbye.

Δ

The next day is Sunday, but Mom disappears into her room to work. Kaya spends most of the day in her room too. I have to lie in wait in the upstairs hallway to catch her on the way back from the washroom.

"Do you remember," I say, "when you were taking those two roses upstairs the day of Dad's funeral?"

Even in the dim light of the hall, I see her eyes go wide and kind of blank.

"It was that man that gave them to you, you said. Mr. Grimsby. That's the man who shot himself."

It takes her a long moment, but at last she nods again, and her eyes, if anything, go wider.

"Why?" I ask.

The story comes out of her almost as if I pushed a button. She doesn't need to think. She just talks. She seems kind of like a great big talking doll. As I listen, I grow sick with dread.

"He had them with him at the funeral," she says. "And I was kind of crying. And he said he was so sorry, and he gave me the roses."

She stops and looks at me. *There*, her eyes say. *Happy?* She moves as if to pass me, but I make a wall, a big fat wall. I keep talking.

"We ran into each other right there on these stairs," I say, pointing. "And I asked you where you got them, and you said that Mr. Grimsby gave them to you." I look at her closely. "It sounded like you knew him." I pause again. "I thought maybe you rode in one of his toy cars like the other kids. But it wasn't that, was it?"

It takes her a moment. She's definitely thinking now. And she's getting mad. "It was at the funeral," she says. "He gave them to me there."

She knows I know she's lying.

"Why are you hassling me about some stupid roses from Dad's funeral?" she says, and shoves past me, almost stepping on me to get to her room. I follow her and listen at the door and hear banging, as if she's drumming her feet on the floor, and great heaving sobs. I want to go in there. I do. I'm too scared, though. What's happening is too big for me. Way too big.

Δ

The next morning, Kaya is gone, suitcase and all.

It's me who realizes it, me who nudges open the door to the empty room, who examines the nest of a bed and judges it un-slept-in, who looks in the closet for Kaya's special suitcase covered in tapestry farm animals and finds it missing.

"She left in the night," I say, frantic and breathless from my rapid journey from bedroom to kitchen. "She's gone. So's her suitcase."

Mom kind of collapses against the kitchen counter, and I watch her dissolve, all tears and confusion. My own body straightens, its shaking stilled.

"We should call the police," I say.

"She never took her suitcase before," Mom says.

I hand her the phone.

"You go off to school now, honey," Mom says after she hangs up. She's got herself under control. "I'm going to talk to the officer who's coming over. Then I'm going to take a drive downtown. Who knows? Maybe I'll find her, pop her in the car and bring her on home."

Mom is taking action like moms are supposed to. I breathe deep, swallow my misery and head upstairs. One thing for sure: I am not going to school.

Δ

I walk along the sidewalk on the other side of the street and try not to look like I'm looking. The house with the taped-off front yard is kind of grungy looking, old stucco, overgrown bushes, dead lawn. Someone's done some sort of gardening since I was here two days ago, though. Pretty extreme gardening, actually. There's a heap of stuff on the lawn, and all the way along the path a row of short stalks stick out of the ground. Every one of the rose bushes has been cut down. That's where he shot himself, I think, and I look for signs of blood even though I know I won't see it from across the street.

I look for signs of life. Nothing. The house looks abandoned, and the yellow tape cordons off the path as well as the yard. I reach the corner, cross and start down the sidewalk on the same side as the house.

Two years ago, the front yard was littered with toys, the rose bushes were covered in blooms, the grass was green and those boys were having a gas.

I pause in front of the house and peer at the lawn, at the path. I still don't see any blood.

I'm lifting the police tape and stepping onto that path when a car comes around the corner. I pay no attention until it speeds up and draws to the curb right behind me, facing the wrong way and screeching just a bit as the driver applies the brakes. The driver is a man and he is out of the car and after me, but I've already dropped the tape and taken off at top speed. This can't be happening. Again!

"You kids make me sick," he shouts, "coming around here peering into corners."

"Dad!" Another voice—a girl's.

I slow down and glance over my shoulder.

His daughter's in the car, but she has the window open and she's leaning out. "Dad!" She almost screams this time. "I'm going to call the police," the man shouts, but at least he has given up the chase. "Can't you people give my father some privacy?"

I've never read the obituary section before, but on Tuesday morning I slip out of bed while Mom is still sleeping, ease open the front door, grab the paper and take it up to my room. Whatever happens, I don't want Mom to start thinking what I'm thinking. Not yet.

There it is, right at the top.

Alan Grimsby: 1919–1998
Survived by his loving companion of forty-three years,
Jennifer Ainsworth, and his four children, David, Adrian,
Cedric, and Charlotte, and seven grandchildren.
The funeral will be held at St. Anselm's Anglican Church,
Saturday, October 3, at 11 a.m.

That's only four days from today. I read and reread, but find few clues. It makes no mention of how he died. No bullet to the brain here. And it says nothing about his life either. Except.

Four children. Which was the shouting man with the daughter?

And what about that "loving companion"?

CHAPTER TEN

Beth

The days that follow pass somehow. Mom goes off in the car every evening, looking, and comes home late every night, exhausted and alone. She calls the Missing Persons Department every day, and learns nothing. We eat what we can scrape together, or order pizza. I spend what's left of my babysitting stash on candy to get me through the long lonely evenings, and I master three new card tricks while I'm eating it. I avoid Jane and Samantha and skip classes, or doze in the back row.

I feel like I'm trapped inside a tunnel. I've decided to go to that funeral, and in the meantime all I can do is shuffle along in the dark. Ideas float into my head, but I hustle them out again. I could talk to Mom, or knock on the door of that house or go downtown myself. But every one of those ideas scares the hell out of me. The funeral scares me too. But I know I can do it. Until then, I'm mastering a really complicated trick shuffle.

On Thursday, Michelle corners me at the end of the hall. "Where's Kaya?" she says.

I can't find it in me to be friendly with this annoying girl, but I do tell her the truth. "Gone," I say. "She ran away last weekend."

Michelle opens her mouth to ask another question, and I cut her short. "Listen, that's all I know. Okay?"

Michelle wanders off looking crushed, and I walk straight out the front door of the school. If I hurry, I can make it home in time for the perfect trio: Häagen-Dazs ice cream (Chocolate Chocolate Chip), the next card trick in my book and my favourite soap (*All My Children*).

Δ

Saturday comes eventually, and Mom's at work, so I don't need an excuse for going out at ten o'clock on a Saturday morning in a black skirt and nylons. I have to take a bus to get to the church, but I still make it there twenty minutes before the service. My second funeral, I think, and I push the memories of funeral number one far, far away.

I take the program from the tall man in black who stands in the doorway, waiting to see if he will ask who I am, but he does not. Other people are coming along behind me and the entranceway is full of people milling about. I'm on the lookout for the shouting son, though I hope he didn't get a good-enough look at me to recognize me here in such different clothes. As it turns out, I hear him before I see him.

"What is this? A circus?"

I freeze and peer through the crowd. It's easy to pick out who is talking because everyone has turned to look. I can only see part of him, but the woman he is addressing is so tall that her pale, pointy face and her smooth dark hair with its tidy line of white roots rise above the crowd. The loving companion. Jennifer Ainsworth.

The loving companion has a strangely serene smile on her face, as if this man's discomfort gives her great pleasure. "No, David," she says slowly, pacing herself. "This is a funeral. Your father's funeral."

"And you had to invite the whole world."

"Lower your voice, David. You're embarrassing yourself."

She stops pitching her voice to the crowd after that, and I hear no more from her, but I hear one more petulant comment from the son. "But I don't want them here," he says.

I turn away and enter the rapidly filling sanctuary. Who are all these people? I wonder, and feel a flash of sympathy for that angry man, sharing his father's funeral with all these strangers. I slip into the back pew. I have a reason for being here, I tell myself, though the man certainly would not approve that reason, and he wouldn't like it if he connected me with the girl on the sidewalk the other day. Straightening my back against the hard wood, I look around.

There's music, but it's only coming from the organ, I realize, and nobody's listening. There's a certain murmuring quality to the crowd, a "we're at the funeral of a man who shot himself" sort of murmuring, though it feels respectful enough. A bit sad, maybe, just as you'd expect.

I turn my gaze to the far side of the church and, to my surprise, it falls upon those boys, the ones I'd seen riding the toy car, Paul and Dave. I stare. And realize quickly that they are not the only ones. Over the next minute or two,

I count seven boys, teenaged and younger; four of them (including Paul and Dave) I recognize from school. They're not in a pack like usual; they are in tidy family groups, sitting between moms and dads, hair neatly combed, shoulders square, jacketed. The boys are not jostling and talking. They are silent, waiting.

Clearly Paul and Dave were not the only ones to hang out with Mr. Grimsby. Boys only, though, I notice.

I don't like the thoughts that come to me, so I turn to the folded paper in my lap. The program or whatever you call it. I open it and smooth it across my thighs. *Alan Samuel Grimsby*, I read. *Grim* indeed, I am thinking, when I'm startled by a body thrusting itself into the pew right next to me.

It's a girl, younger than me, with a familiar face. From the neighbourhood, for sure. Why does she look so terrified? Like a rabbit cornered by a wolverine. And the name comes to me.

Diana.

"I think you know my sister," I say. "Didn't you and Kaya—?"

But I don't get a chance to finish the question.

"I'm sorry. I, uh, I think I see . . ." the girl stammers, and rushes from her seat.

A strange darkness runs through me. Something is very, very wrong, and I'm pretty sure I know what it is.

Δ

The service starts soon after, but I find it hard to pay attention at first. Diana is perched at the end of a pew three rows up, and I'm watching the back of her head. Her neck has a tilt to it that is not quite right. Tears gather in the back of my nose.

The priest drones on. The congregation stands. The congregation sits. The congregation prays. The priest warns us all away from a life of sin, offers up a clean, pure path to heaven. Suggests Alan Samuel Grimsby is currently on that very path. I hold in a snort and wonder about the church's position on suicide. Not to mention whatever else . . .

From what the priest says, it sounds like the ashes in the urn up there at the front came from the body of a man who died peacefully at the end of a long life, well lived. Around me, people listen, heads bowed or eyes trained politely on the speaker. No one seems bothered by the lie. Except for me. And Diana, I'm guessing.

Lies, I should say.

Then the loving companion gets up, and every head in the room straightens. She weeps as she speaks. "I still remember the first time I came to the house in Montreal," she says, and has to stop to blow her nose before she can continue. "The toys! He was an antiques dealer back then, but he had such a love for the toys that I don't know how many he ever sold. He brought them home instead. The kids loved them. Just loved them." Another long sniff. "I see others here who enjoyed Alan's kindness and generosity, even as an old man." She looks at Paul and Dave and the rest. "He loved the children. Always did."

I watch her looking at the boys, exulting in the goodness of the man she is remembering, her part in his good works. I feel as if I am seeing right inside her skull.

Then I see her see Diana.

And even from the back, I see Diana being seen.

Diana shrinks down in the pew as if she would fold her shoulders together and disappear. And the loving companion stops talking abruptly. Grief takes her over completely. At least it looks like grief.

The angry son rises in the front row and strides toward the pulpit. His hand is on her elbow. The priest stands behind them, looking nervous. The angry son pulls at the loving companion's arm, and everyone hears when he hisses, "That's enough, Jennifer. Sit down."

But she has something else to say, through her tears, right into the microphone so everyone can hear. "You're the one who did it to him, David," she cries, "forbidding an old man his grandchildren."

He hustles her out then, and everyone can hear their shouting voices, though we can't make out any more words. I look around for those poor deprived grandchildren, maybe including the girl who shouted "Dad" from the car window, but I don't think they're here. Diana remains folded up in her seat.

The priest steps up and continues where he left off. He has nothing to say about what has just happened in his church.

As the service ends and the organ music ushers everyone to their feet, I slip into the foyer ahead of the crowd, make my way outside and wait there, determined. Diana has something to tell and I am going to drag it out of her. I push those folded shoulders—that frightened face—out of my mind. Somebody's got to put words to this.

I peer in the door and see the family members all in a row: the receiving line. The loving companion is nowhere in sight.

I hated the receiving line at Dad's funeral. I loathed standing next to Mom, the whispered words, the scratchy, perfumed hugs, the sympathy, thick and clotted, like sour milk. I hated Kaya all spread out drawing swans in a corner, off the hook as always.

A voice at my elbow. "You just skulk around everywhere, don't you."

It's the girl from the angry son's car. She's tall, skinny, with beady, deep-set eyes and an oversized mouth. She's not just the girl from the car. She's from school too, I realize, just as she draws back and says, "I know you. You're that girl who hangs out at the end of the hall."

"My name's Beth," I say.

"Marlene," the girl says. Then, "Why were you lurking around outside my grandfather's house that day?"

Grandfather. Formal.

I don't like the word *lurking* but have no answer. My mouth is probably hanging open like a fish's. That's when I see Diana leave the church. She does not pause, she does not look. She strides through the scattered bodies, and she's gone.

Marlene follows my gaze. "Hey! She goes to our school too, doesn't she?" She does an exaggerated double take. Paul and Dave are following two sets of parents into the parking lot. "And so do they. What's going on? What were you all doing in there?" Her initial bluster is gone. She seems to have trouble getting the next sentence out. "*I* wasn't even in there."

I wonder if Marlene is going to cry. I kind of hope she does, actually. She's ignorant and bossy. She *deserves* to cry.

Your grandfather hurt my sister, I think, trying the words on. I imagine the words as sound, vibrating Marlene's eardrums, reaching her brain. What if I shouted them out? What if they could vibrate every eardrum around?

Your grandfather hurt my sister.

My mouth opens. Words come out. "He had that big toy car," I say. "And I think he had other stuff too. A lot of kids hung out there and played with that stuff."

Marlene looks at me and I can tell that she's not satisfied. "What about you?" she says. "Are you here because you liked to play in my grandfather's toy car?"

The angry son comes out then. "Marlene," he calls before he reaches the bottom step, "get in the car. We're going."

The loving companion, who has appeared from somewhere, is reaching for him, trying to pull him back. "But, the reception," she says. Then her gaze lights on me. "Get out of here!" she shouts, the words bursting out through a sob. "I can't take another minute of you girls. Not one more minute. If it wasn't for you . . ."

After a terrifying moment, my limbs thaw and I lumber off, past the bus stop and along the boulevard toward home. I keep up the pace until I'm over the rise and out of sight.

CHAPTER ELEVEN

Beth

On the very last day of Dad's life, Mom dragged Kaya and me to his bedside in the hospital. Kaya held Dad's hand. I didn't want to go near him. He was unconscious and twitchy and his skin was thin and his bones stuck out. There was a smell. And all those tubes.

Mom sort of hovered, but not in a loving way exactly. Nurses came and went and were kind. Dad made big groaning sounds twice, and shifted in the bed. Once he swore loudly and Mom pushed the button on his morphine dispenser. I would have liked a morphine dispenser of my own that day.

Then Mom was standing over the bed, arms crossed on her chest, tears pouring down her face in a way that I had not known that tears could pour, especially Mom's. "Your father's dying, Beth," she said through gritted teeth. "Get over here and say goodbye."

Kaya was sitting quietly on a chair pulled up right beside the bed, bent over with her head on the sheet and her arms reached out holding Dad's hand. She was murmuring something, something strange most likely. And she was ignoring both of us.

I forced myself to cross the room and stand up against the bed. Kaya did not look up. I let an arm reach out and hover above the sheet near Dad's knee. I let it brush the cotton, the merest whiff of a touch.

"Goodbye, Dad," I murmured.

Mom made a humphing sound through her tears.

After that, there were hours more to get through.

I slept through a lot of it, in a big chair in the corner, and left the room as often as I could to get stuff from the vending machine. Once Kaya and I went together to the cafeteria and ate burgers and fries off heavy china.

We stayed the night, which was weird and terrible. Kaya slept in the second bed in the room, which wasn't occupied. I slept as best I could in that big chair. And Mom just kind of stood, at least at first. I jolted awake at one point to the sight of her lying full-length along the edge of Dad's bed, her head in the crook of his neck, her arm across his chest. I closed my eyes, tight, and opened them again. She was murmuring something. I drifted back to sleep, thinking. That was probably the one and only time I ever saw Mom touch Dad except for a shoulder hug or peck on the cheek or lips sometimes, or the necessary touching of the last year when Dad was really sick. Maybe there had been something between them once, long ago. Maybe I was seeing the leftovers from that.

I must have slept for a long time. The next time I woke, I stayed still, watching Mom through my eyelashes, afraid to move. She was still stretched out on the bed with Dad, but now she was asleep.

At last Kaya rolled over, sat up, brought her hands to her face and said, "Mom?"

Mom was up and off that bed in an instant, like a teenager caught making out with her boyfriend on the couch.

She collected herself quickly, turning back to Dad on the bed. She touched his face, his neck, and took a great, heaving breath.

"He's gone," she said.

Kaya let out a sob and ran to her, and Mom let her press up against her and cry. She even laid an arm across Kaya's back. But she did not hug her. I got up out of the chair and went and stood looking down at my father.

He's dead, I thought.

Δ

To me, Dad's funeral was just as awful as Mr. Grimsby's, even though there was no yelling, and there were no crazy people like that loving companion and the angry son. No mysterious granddaughter waited outside either. Dad's funeral was just family and friends gathered together, sad but polite, a few rituals, a song, maybe two.

I wore a dark blue outfit that I pulled out of the back of my closet. Too tight. Scratchy. A perfect match for how I was feeling. Kaya emerged in pink and purple, all floaty looking. I remembered that Dad had commented on that very outfit just a month ago, told her she looked like a princess or something. He'd hate the bunchy blue thing I was wearing, I thought, if he even noticed. I bit back a snarky comment.

She had a small bag over her shoulder with paper sticking out the top.

"You're bringing that?" I said.

"Yes."

I glared at her, but it didn't seem to make any difference. Oh well. At least it ruined her outfit. And maybe Mom would say something.

At the funeral home, a very serious man I had never seen before led us to the front row. I sat beside Mom and stared at the urn, which was on a white tablecloth on a table up front, beside where the minister—was he actually a minister?—stood.

"What's that?" Kaya asked, following my eyes.

"Nothing," I said.

Kaya stared up at me and her eyes flashed wide and filled with tears, but I really truly did not care.

I was not going to tell my sister that Dad was in that urn. I didn't even want to think about it myself. Flashes of bubbling, melting flesh and cracking bones erupted in my mind, and no mental effort seemed to stop them. A proper coffin with a body in it would be much easier somehow. I didn't listen to the minister or to my uncle, and I only mouthed the words to the songs.

Later we stood with Mom, and all the people walked past us in a line and hugged us one by one. There were a number of strangers, so I didn't think much of the tall, dark-haired woman and the elderly man with a cane and a British accent. I let the woman kiss my cheek and express her sympathy.

"I'm Jennifer," she said. "I'm so sorry for your loss."

I let the man take my hand in his. "And I'm Mr. Grimsby," he said. "Alan Grimsby." His hand was cool and dry.

Behind us, my twelve-year-old sister was spread out on the floor with her paper and her coloured pencils. She must have seen Mr. Grimsby in the line, but I didn't see how she reacted. I do remember looking back at her at one point. I was furious at her for getting out of the line, for being a kid.

She was drawing a swan. It was huge, crooked and smudgy, taking up a whole sheet of paper, which she had unfolded to fill the space in front of her. When I looked at her, she refolded the paper.

Later, in the car, she held the wad of paper in her lap, along with the box of coloured pencils.

My hand lighted on the paper, almost without my willing it, my thumb sliding underneath to take the sheets from her. "Can I see?" I said casually.

I yelped as her arm came down hard on my hand.

"*Girls*," Mom said, her voice strange, thick.

I leaned toward Kaya and dropped my voice to a whisper. "You don't have to show them to me. I'm just curious what sort of pictures a kid draws at her father's funeral. You're not a baby anymore, you know."

She clutched the drawings, refusing to look at me.

"Mom said I didn't even have to come," she hissed. "You heard her."

She angled her face away from me and clenched her jaw. Mine was clenched too, but I held my gaze on her—and she knew it, even if she wouldn't look.

Δ

Unlike Kaya, I had to help out at the reception we held at our house. Food had to be unwrapped and put out, drinks offered. When I went into the living room later on to put out dishes of nuts, I found Kaya perched on the end of the couch, watching the front door. There was an intensity about her that bothered me, but then, everything about her was bothering me that day.

As I hovered in the doorway, Mom crossed the room and bent over Kaya, gathered her into a hug and buried her face in her hair. Kaya raised her arms politely and placed them on Mom's back. I watched Mom's shoulders heave. At last two of Mom's friends gathered round her, pulling her off Kaya and into their arms, where she cried some more. Kaya shook herself off and looked, once again, at the front door. I put the nuts down and headed back to the kitchen, but Kaya shoved past me before I got there, and I watched her head out onto the back deck, where the smokers were.

After that, I don't remember noticing her until later, on the stairs. She was on her way up, cheeks flushed, hair extra curly with damp ends, and she was holding two orange rose-buds on short stems.

She couldn't get past me, so I had her captive for a moment. "Where'd those come from?" I asked. "You went out somewhere, didn't you. Where?"

She looked up at me. "I was here," she said.

"But who gave those to you?"

"Nobody," she said.

"Did you take them?"

"No. They're mine."

She was clutching them tight, and her whole face was gathered up into pure possession.

Something in me must have been equally determined. "Then who gave them to you?" I asked again.

"Mr. Grimsby," she said.

At the church, I hadn't recognized the bent-over man leaning on a cane, but when Kaya said his name, I found myself back on the corner of Discovery and Fourteenth, letting him take my hand in his. *I'm Mr. Grimsby*, he had said.

"I didn't think he came to the house," I said as Kaya tried to wedge herself past me up the narrow stairs.

"He gave them to me at the church," she said. "Let me by."

And I did. I let her and her roses pass me on the stairs. I abandoned my curiosity and went back to resenting her as I said goodbye to guest after guest and helped Mom clean up.

∆

Two years have passed since then. Another funeral. Shoplifting. Juvenile detention. Running away. Drugs, I'm pretty sure. The word *prostitution* keeps floating into my mind.

Mr. Grimsby's the key to all of it, I know it, but he's dead, and Kaya's gone, and Mom's posters and midnight searches seem to be getting us nowhere.

I need a plan.

CHAPTER TWELVE

Kaya

Mom gives you a run for your money. So do the police, since you've broken your probation, which makes those first couple of weeks kind of tricky. Not to mention the bloody, brain-spattered nightmares.

The worst moment, though, the one that sends you straight into oblivion, is the poster.

You plan to go straight for Sarah when you get down there. You're ready to tell her the whole story, or big parts of it. She'll help you once she knows. She won't just shove you onto the next bus.

Before you reach Princess Avenue, though, you run into Jim.

He takes one look at you dragging that silly suitcase covered in lambs and chickens, and he knows you're easy pickings. Next thing you know, you're back in his room with a needle in your arm. He climbs on top of you, paying himself back, you suppose, but you hardly care, you feel so good. That's the thing of it: people can hurt you; people can reject you, neglect you, die on you; people can even blow their brains out without thinking of you—and if you can get your hands on some heroin, none of it matters. It all floats away, even a heavy unwashed body right on top of you, a grubby hand yanking your clothes out of the way . . . even that doesn't really matter. Not all that much.

Jim keeps you close this time. He brings the men in. He tosses greasy McDonald's takeout bags of food onto the bed.

When you ask about Sarah, he shrugs. "Sarah who?"

He doesn't lock you in, though, or handcuff you to the bed, and one afternoon when you're alone, you dig around in your suitcase for some clean clothes, get dressed and head out. You'll come back within an hour, you think as you open the door to the street—before he gets back, long before you start shaking and puking.

The crisp air brings instant tears, as the world, the real place where you're standing—Earth—compels you, woos you with a stunted tree, a few red leaves still hanging on, with the blue sky, when you look up, with a dog's face in the window of a car, tongue lolling.

You gulp, and take off down the street at a good clip. Candy, you're thinking, some of those Pocky sticks would be so good. And a Coke. You managed to scrabble together almost five dollars. The closest store is right on Hastings, on the corner. The man behind the counter does not smile at you, but he's not exactly rude either. He nods as he takes your money, gives you change. You step around the corner, off Hastings, and open your Coke, enjoying the fizzy sound, anticipating the first cold, sweet swig. You have your head tilted back, the can to your mouth, when you see her.

Sarah.

She is staring out at you, smiling brightly, from a small white poster behind the bars in the store window. *Missing*, the poster says. You stand there looking for a long time.

Then you shove the Pocky sticks in your pocket, drop the Coke in a garbage can and start walking east down Hastings, past Main. You're breathless by the time you arrive and your body is starting to long for a fix, but you ignore it.

When you turn onto Princess, you stop, awestruck. The grey house, rundown as ever, is all garden now. Two huge sunflowers rise from pots on either side of the never-used front door, and between the two houses, some sort of vines are strung up. You stare. Beans. A couple of enormous beans still hang from the plants. Another sort of vine with round-ish leaves and red and yellow flowers trails along the ground. Nasturtiums. You feel a moment's pleasure at your knowledge of the name, before you remember that you learned it from Mr. G.

You duck and weave round the house, through the bean plants, and climb the steps. This time you don't hesitate. You bang away with all your strength.

"Charlie!" you call out.

He comes. The door opens.

He looks at you. "Aren't you supposed to be in jail?" he says, but not in a mean way.

"Where's Sarah?" you ask, your voice sharp.

He stares for a moment, and his crumbly body crumbles a little more. Then he starts to close the door in your face. "Hey, take yourself off, kid," he says.

"Where is she?" you say again, softening your expression and your voice.

"I don't know," he says. "A lot of people have been asking. The police were even here last week." He pauses. "Took them long enough."

"How long's it been?" you ask, reaching up to wipe a sudden sheet of sweat off your forehead.

"Couple months," he replies. He seems to take pity on you. "Hey, come on in. I can give you a little something."

He doesn't seem to expect anything from you in exchange for the drugs, though really it's a pretty small hit. It just stops the sweats and the shaking.

"Come here," he says. "I want to show you."

You find yourself in the battered living room, where some guy is on the nod on the couch, with that same scrawny kitten, now larger and scrawnier, curled up on his back. Those prowling ghostly cats in the park flash into your mind.

In front of you is a door with an open padlock hanging off it: Sarah's room, where you slept that one night. Charlie opens the door and ushers you in. You have visions of Bluebeard's chamber, awash with blood and hung with dead wives, but you step through the doorway and look around.

"I showed the cop," he says, "but he wasn't all that interested."

The room is a mess, jammed with stuff, clothes mixed with junk. They are shoved onto shelves, heaped on the bed, the floor. A closet at the end of the room stands mostly empty, just a few metal hangers, a dressing gown trailing crookedly from one of them.

"I don't know what to do with all this," he says. It doesn't sound as if he's annoyed. He sounds kind of lost. "She hadn't really been living here for a while," he adds. "Listen, do you think there's anything here you might like?"

Dread, black and bitter, floods your belly. You know it's naive, but you say, "It's hers. She'll want it when she gets back."

He stares at the wall and nods slowly. "Well. Yes."

You know what he's thinking. And you kind of know he's right.

Δ

A week later, in early October, you wake up against the wall in a tumble of dirty sheets and ratty blankets. Three other girls are crammed into the bed with you, one of them along the bottom, so you have to keep your feet tucked up out of her face.

You got away from Jim, suitcase in tow. You didn't go home, though. You will not go home.

You're lucky to have a room at all. Most won't rent to kids without an adult around, even one night at a time, but you can usually find someone who knows your money's as good as anyone else's, someone willing to take the risk. And the four of you have been sharing, saving on rent and keeping each other safe.

"Rise and shine," you say.

Within an hour, the bunch of you are taking over the corner table by the window in the nearest McDonald's, Egg McMuffins, hash browns, coffee and orange juice for all, the manager watching you from behind the counter.

You gulp at your coffee and burn your tongue. Look around. You're getting tired of being out here. The grind is wearing at you. And the more time goes by, the more you know that there is something that you have to do, though you do not want to do it.

It's been weeks since that night when you took off from home. It's fall now. It rains a lot. And you find yourself thinking, more than you used to, about how worried they must be. Mom and Beth. You called once, got no answer, and hung up without leaving a message. You've seen more posters, of Sarah. Pictures of other girls too. And a couple of you. You're not missing, though. You just have a really, really stubborn mother.

Is that where you belong? That house, with Beth stuffing herself and Mom learning every little thing about the human psyche . . . Not yours, though. She doesn't know a damn thing about yours.

You dip your golden hash brown into ketchup and take a small bite. Your heart beats in your chest.

Breakfast done, you go back to your room to get ready for work, which is quite a production, especially with the sickness kicking in, the price you pay for sleep and relaxing over breakfast. Still, you look good when you're done. One of the girls—it's Amber, actually, the one you punched way back in the spring—comes with you, and you head down to the back streets by the tracks, where you can stay out of sight of the police. They'll pick you up just because of your age, which is so unfair.

You stand kitty-corner to each other on what people call the kiddy stroll. *Kitty. Kiddy.* You smile, feeling strong, kicked up by the chase. Amber breaks first—a bald guy in a pale blue hatchback. You stride back and forth on your corner, oozing confidence. A couple of cars slow as they pass, but they don't stop. Amber doesn't come back. Two girls in the back of a loaded Honda jeer at you, and your stride slows. You kick at a post and stub your toe, swipe at the tear that's suddenly there on your cheek. Bitches.

That's when the red pickup slows down beside you. You approach. It's small, a bit battered but clean, and the guy behind the wheel looks youngish, clean-shaven, kind of good-looking, with short blond hair, a smile with no leer to it. He cocks his head at you.

"Going my way?" he says.

Wow. Original.

You shrug your shoulders and get in. Which is stupid. You know that. You've learned to negotiate through car windows. *How much? What? Where?* And while you're negotiating, you scope out the guy and the car. You check in with yourself. What do your instincts tell you? You glance in the back. Could someone be hiding in there? Are there weapons or anything at all that could be used to hurt you or to restrain you? Not that any of that guarantees safety, but jumping in with no check at all is just plain dumb. And today that's what you tell yourself over and over again.

You have lots of time to berate yourself because the car keeps going, east. He ignores you when you say you don't want to leave the neighbourhood.

"Hey, I know a place," he says, and that quiets you for a few blocks, though your gut is anything but quiet.

Your gut shouts at you. *Get out. Get out right now.* But this guy's instincts are way better than yours because just as you reach for the door handle to jump at the next red light, you hear the click. He's locked the doors.

And somehow you're on a highway now, going fast, no lights in sight, nobody to call out to for help. Would they help if you did? you wonder.

"Let me out," you say.

"I know a place," he says again.

"I'll call the police," you say.

And he scoffs, half laugh, half damp clearing of the throat.

You go quiet, thinking hard, waiting for your chance. Either it will come or it won't.

You think about all you've been through. You think, for a moment, about Beth and Mom. Push those thoughts away. You'll escape, and they'll never need to know about this.

Mr. Grimsby flashes into your head and you shove him out again. Now is not the time for whining and moaning about your past. If you don't think of something fast, you're not going to have a future.

Δ

Well, he does know a place: a gravel parking lot along a logging road, just up the rise from a suburb of some sort.

Your first strategy is a weak one. As soon as he clicks the doors unlocked, you're off, running for the bush in your high heels. Of course he catches you. What happens next is bad, but through it all you're on the alert, and as he shifts from beating to rape, you take your chance, fingernails clawing at his right eyeball, knee coming up into his balls with all the force you've got.

He shouts and thrusts you away, and you add your own momentum to the thrust and hurtle into the thick brush at the downhill edge of the parking lot. He's after you fast, but you're a lot smaller than he is: you can push through the bush more easily. You find yourself on a steep slope, and you kick off your shoes and head down, running, walking, tumbling, letting gravity work in your favour. He's thrashing around behind you, shouting nasty stuff.

When the distance between you grows, you stop and listen. You don't hear anything, and for a moment you feel something like relief. Then you realize he's quiet because he's listening too. So you move silently, easing yourself off to the left, against the slope, looking for a spot to hide and wait him out.

After a while, he shouts again. You hold your silence. He ventures farther down, loud and mad. And stops again. More silence.

Your back is braced against a tree. Your knees are pulled up to your chest. You've got bare, scraped-up feet; bruised ribs, maybe broken. A battered face. One of your nails is ripped back from your finger. Your clothes are torn. It's getting dark, but at least you have your jacket.

You breathe deep, ignoring the pain in your side. Minutes tick by. Maybe hours. You don't know how much time passes, but you do know that you don't want to spend the night huddled against a tree in the bush.

At last a wild commotion of movement and sound arises from the man's hiding place. You can't see him, but you can hear him and you can sense him, on his feet, a tsunami of fury pouring off him down the slope. More obscenities.

"I'll find you!" he shouts. "You think you can go back to your life, but I'll be there. I'll come after you!"

And as you hear him thundering his way back up the slope, as you hear the truck's engine turn over, as you hear the truck tear out of the parking lot and down the road not far from your tree, your silent breathing turns to loud sobbing. You stifle the tears fast, though. You've got to get onto that road now, while you can still find it.

It's a long journey back downtown. You make it to the road right off, and down the hill into town, though it's pretty hard on your bare feet. You find out you're in Port Moody, not that that's much help. You have no money and no choice. You get yourself onto a main road and stick out your thumb. A guy stops right off. You don't like the look of him, but what can you do? You get in. You give him what he wants. And you huddle back against the door, trying to keep the nausea down while he drives you home.

Δ

The other girls cover you for a couple of days while you start to heal. And for the first time since you came back downtown, you want to write. You find a stack of napkins from McDonald's and a couple of pencil crayons. You fill those napkins with the scrinchiest writing you can muster, so small only you can read it. And you tell what happened to you. The man. The drive. The beating. The escape. The journey back. Every little detail makes it onto those napkins. You read them over and over to yourself. You imagine you're reading them to Sarah, and every time you draw her into your mind, you hear those words: *They could be me. They could be you.*

When you're done, you wander outside in the rain and drop the stack of napkins into the gutter, stand and watch the ink run, the napkins swirling away, some sticking to the curb, some not. You give the sticky ones a push with your foot, until every bit of paper is gone.

Then you go back inside and start caking makeup onto your bruises. It's time to go to work.

You stay away from the kiddy stroll now. You've been thinking about it, and you've decided to give Sarah's corner a try. Princess and Hastings. Yes, the police will pick you up if they see you, but you've got a sharp eye and good spotters. And you're more afraid of the guy in the pickup than you are of the police. He won't look for you on Hastings. You're pretty sure.

You do a good job of avoiding the police, but the second afternoon out there, you glance up and catch Beth staring at you from the window of a passing bus.

CHAPTER THIRTEEN

Beth

The day after the funeral, I take the Hastings bus downtown. It runs all the way from near my house to downtown and along Hastings to Burnaby. Easy enough. If I want to, I can just stay on it and it will turn around at the end of its route and bring me home again. I'm not getting off downtown, I know that much. I'll just look out the window. I'll look and look. That's all.

And if I see her . . . ? I have no idea what I'll do if I see her.

I don't see her. Not that day. Or the next, Monday, after school. Or the one after that. Mom's working, so she doesn't even know that I don't get home until six most days.

After a week, I get braver. I get off the bus just past the scary part, get a bus back, get off downtown and head east again. I can go back and forth three or four times in an afternoon that way.

Another week passes. Still, I don't see her.

One day I decide to skip school. Maybe she's never out

on the street in the late afternoon. Maybe I'm just missing her every single day. So, on Tuesday morning I'm on the bus by nine thirty. Back and forth I go. Back and forth. At lunchtime I get myself a milkshake and a burger. No eating on the bus, the driver says, so I sit on the bus-stop bench and wolf it down. Back and forth.

I'm on my way back downtown when I see her, standing right there on the corner, teetering on her high-heeled boots. I lurch up out of my seat, and collapse right back into it, fighting the urge to scream, *Stop this bus!* Instead, I check the time and the place. *Princess and Hastings, northwest corner. Half past one.*

As soon as I feel like I'm in a safe part of downtown, I get off the bus and cross the street. *Go home*, I tell myself. *Or call Mom.* But Mom's picking up some night shifts, nursing, this week, so she sleeps all afternoon. I know it doesn't matter if I wake her up; she'd want to know. She'd come. But I'm not ready for that. I need to see Kaya again.

Back I go on the bus. And there she is: same corner; same teetering sister. Half an hour later, I pass the corner again and she's gone.

My transfer is running out. I'll need to pay again. I should go home. I should call Mom. I don't. Scraping together every last dime at the bottom of my purse, I buy my way onto another eastbound bus. Princess and Hastings comes. And goes. No Kaya. I look at my watch. Three o'clock. This time, I let the bus take me all the way to the end of the line, asking myself, *If she's there, will I get off?*

It's way past four when the bus approaches the corner again. The driver actually tried to make me get off at the bus loop in Burnaby, but I just said that I had slept past my stop, and he relented. I sit up straight in my seat, tip my head against the cool glass of the window and put all of my will into looking, as if my gaze can pull my sister up out of the sidewalk. Magic.

And maybe I'm more powerful than I think I am, because there she is. There she is, and this time, she's looking right at me. Our gazes lock. As the bus passes, I turn my whole body and look back. She's still staring, but she has not moved from the spot. The bus pulls into the stop. *Get up!* I shout inside my head. But I don't. Two people get off, four get on, one of them with a stroller; many seconds tick by. I do not get up, and Kaya does not move.

At last the bus carries on its way. Our gaze is broken. I sit in my seat and shake all the way home.

Δ

It's past five when I get there, and Mom's up, slouched over the kitchen table with a mug of tea. She jumps to her feet when I tell her what happened.

"Let's go," she says.

On the drive, she asks questions. When I tell her about all my bus trips, she looks at me hard. "Smart girl," she says when I explain why I didn't get off.

Princess and Hastings is deserted when we drive by, so we park the car and walk the neighbourhood. I know Mom's been doing this, but I never have, and I don't like it. I keep my body pulled in tight and don't meet anyone's eyes.

Mom is silent until she stops in front of a window right

near that corner. I look up. SHEWAY, the sign says, VANCOUVER NATIVE HEALTH SOCIETY. Mom points. And my gaze is drawn to a small poster on the inside of the window looking out. *Have you seen Kaya?* the poster says. She squints out at us from a photo Mom took in August. Underneath the picture, our phone number. And another line of text: *Kaya, please come home.*

She has called twice, and the second time, she left a message. Somehow she always catches us out. *I'm okay*, she said. *Don't worry about me.* As if that were possible.

"She was standing right over there three hours ago," I say, pointing. "Right over there. She must have seen the poster herself."

"I put up lots," Mom says.

"I know, Mom. I'm not blind," a voice says.

We both jump and turn, and there she is, her hood shading her face.

"Kaya!" Mom says, and steps forward, arms outstretched, but Kaya moves away from the hug, not into it. Her eyes are stones. Damp stones, but still.

"Leave me alone, can't you?" she says. "Just leave me the fuck alone." Her voice is louder on the repeat. Shrill. She turns and strides away, in sneakers now and tattered jeans.

"Kaya," Mom says again. She does not run after her, though, and neither do I.

I don't know about Mom, but I'm feeling a little bit afraid. That girl is supposed to be my sister, but she feels so far away from me right now. She seems tough in a way that I've never seen before. Harder than ever. Mom and I walk slowly back to the car and drive home.

That night, I'm pretty sure I don't sleep at all. By morning, I have new resolve. She can turn herself to granite, but we're still her family, and she's still ours. I'm going to bring her back to us.

∆

They're all at school the next morning: Jane and Samantha, Diana and Michelle. Since the funeral, I've been ignoring my friends, telling them I'm busy, letting them know it has something to do with Kaya.

Now that I have a plan, I look for Diana first, even though she frightens me. I find her outside with her friends. She pulls away from them as soon as she sees the expression on my face.

"Is Kaya all right?" she asks.

"Yes," I say back, even though I want to ask questions. How does she know my sister? What does she know about her? Well, I sort of want to ask those questions. Really, I know all I need to. Kaya is downtown for the same reason that Diana was at that funeral.

"I want to go get her," I tell Diana. "I want us to go get her together."

"I'll come," she says instantly.

We approach Michelle next. She's coming out of math class, eyes clear, shoulders back, hair gleaming. It's a bit of a shock to see her looking so great. It almost makes me mad, with my sister in such rough shape. She's hesitant when I tell her what we want.

"Look," I say, "as far as I know you're Kaya's only friend. Can't you help her out?"

"I stay away from downtown these days," she says. The pause is long. "But, yes, I'll come."

"Well now, quite the little gathering," says another voice, warm and round, an *I'm-here! Now-step-aside* kind of a voice. Jane has arrived, Samantha in position right behind her.

So we head for the front door of the school in a group of five.

"What's going on?" a voice calls before we reach the front hall.

I stop moving. Turn. It's Marlene.

"You show up outside my granddad's house, you barge in on his funeral," she says. She doesn't seem to care that we are standing in the middle of the hallway, that Michelle and Samantha and Jane are all listening, that her voice is collapsing in on itself. She turns to Diana. "And you. You were there too. You slunk off." She pauses, almost gasps for breath.

I stand, still and quiet, looking at her, not sure. Then it comes. Fury.

"It's none of your business," I say. "Just stay away from us." My eyes make a tunnel through the air between us, locking onto hers, shutting everyone else out.

"It's not my business," she echoes, sounding disbelieving.

A hand grasps my arm, pulls. I yank back and find myself in a tug-of-war with Diana. "We're going to get her sister," Diana says to Marlene. "Are you going to come or not?"

Electricity sparks among us, every which way. I can't believe what I'm hearing. "She can't come," I say, but my voice comes out croaky.

"What do you mean? Where is she?" Marlene asks.

"She ran away," Diana says. She hesitates. "Because of

your grandfather." Diana is standing straight as anything, staring into Marlene's eyes.

Marlene steps back again, eyes on the ground.

I pull myself together. An old man hurt my sister, and he's dead now. This girl has done nothing wrong.

"She's downtown. Hastings Street," I say. "Let's go."

CHAPTER FOURTEEN

Kaya

You're standing on Sarah's corner. She's long gone, but it's still hers: her picture is on the poster in the corner-store window behind you.

Your ribs and your feet are still sore from last week, but makeup pretty much covers the bruises. As for getting into cars again after that, funny how withdrawal can make just about any risk seem worth it. Sure, you're scared, but the move to Hastings was smart: you haven't seen that red pickup truck once. You're tired after a sleepless night, but back on track.

Or you were. Until you saw Beth on that bus, and two hours later, Mom.

And now six girls are coming toward you.

You have no chance to disappear, because they're already waving, or Beth is. Jane is pushing the button for the light, all business. Samantha's holding back a bit. Typical. Michelle is waving at you too, all cheery enthusiasm. What happened to her? You don't want to look at Diana. You don't want her to be here, the light changed now, crossing the street. But you are looking. What else can you do? Anyway, Diana seems kind of stiff—surprise, surprise. And there's one more girl . . .

Who is she?

As they come closer, you recognize that girl from school and a memory flickers, an unwelcome one.

Δ

You were in that place. That place that's been haunting your every move since you came back downtown. A girl was there with her dad, and Mr. G was pleading, kind of. The dad was Mr. G's son.

"Please," Mr. G was saying. "She's my granddaughter."

"Marion's not having it," the dad said. "I just brought Marlene here to say goodbye."

The girl wandered over to the table where you were doing crafts with Jennifer. "What are you making?" she asked, and you were pleased, happy to show and tell, but her dad whisked her away.

As he opened the front door, you saw him gesture toward you and heard him ask, "Does her mother know she's here?" He sounded nervous, as if it was hard to say those words. He had his arm around the girl, his daughter. He hustled her out the door.

Δ

Marlene. Part of you feels amused. You could laugh. Maybe. Here come your chickens. Home to roost.

You imagine making flapping motions with your arms.

You consider turning and running for your life. How could Beth collect these people up and come marching into your world? You take a peek inside yourself and make sure that the reservoir of misery is shut up tight, not one drip, not one drop, oozing out of it, not even a bit of damp at the seal. You inhale, deep, and blow the air out in a long stream. They're on your side of the street now. This is where, if you were in a war, the commander would yell "Fire!" and both sides would send off a volley of bullets: bodies would fall, blood would spatter and the smell of gore and gunpowder, the sounds of human agony, would be everywhere.

But these girls did not come to hurt you, you remind yourself. And, really, you don't want to hurt them either.

Diana comes straight to you, almost shoving Beth and Marlene (how did Marlene come into this?) and Michelle aside. She puts her hand on your arm, and you flinch.

"We've got to talk," she says.

The words are like tiny crowbars. They find that reservoir seal and go at it.

The other girls hustle up behind Diana. You fix your eyes on Beth's face in a last attempt to save yourself. Beth's eyes lock with yours for a moment, slip away and lock again. She *knows*, you think. It's a sickening thought. With it, one of the seals gives way; a leak springs. Another minute and you'll be drowning from the inside out.

"Come on," Diana says, her voice all urgency.

"What are you doing?" Beth says to Diana, then to you, "Kaya, come on home."

Diana's plan, it seems, is hers alone. The others just want

to get you out of here, but you're nowhere near ready to march onto a bus with this crowd.

Diana grabs your elbow and tugs. You stumble forward. A stumble leads to a step; a step leads to another. And the other girls follow along in a bunch, mumbling to each other. Diana leads the way down the street right past the bus stop to a set of church stairs. They are empty except for a body-shaped sleeping bag up against the church door. The bag rises and falls slightly as the body inside it breathes. A shopping cart full of earthly possessions has been pushed up to the wall at the bottom of the steps. The church itself is shut up tight. Diana marches halfway up the stairs and sits you down beside her. She looks at the others, who have followed. They're at the bottom of the steps, all except Beth, who's right behind you.

"I need to talk with Kaya," Diana says.

Beth stares. At her. At you.

You sit right up against Diana's coat, your arm now linked with hers. Moments tick by before you nod at Beth. She leans in a bit, seems about to speak; then she descends and joins the huddle on the sidewalk.

Diana turns to you. She's shaking. And you know precisely why. Or you think you do.

"I'm so sorry," she says, and you feel confusion take over your face, crinkling your forehead, tightening your cheeks.

Sorry?

You see her see your confusion, and you try to interpret what shows on her face then. Relief? Doubt? It takes her a long time to speak again.

"Because of what happened. It's . . . it's my fault."

"It . . ." you say, because what does that even mean? *It*.

And that's when she says the word. Later you find out that she's saying it for the very first time in her whole entire life. Her body, her muscles, her breath, her brain, her heart: all together forming the word that has a chance to save you both, though you don't know that yet. "Abuse."

Once the word is spoken, you parrot it back to her and you stare at each other in horror. What now? You don't notice yourself disentangling your body and edging away, but you realize moments later that a space has opened up and Diana is looking down at the stretch of cement between you, and tears are gushing down her face.

You clutch at the cement step behind you, clench your teeth at the nails-on-chalkboard sensation and feel a fingernail break. Rage wells.

Beth and Marlene and Michelle are staring up at you now. Jane and Samantha are talking urgently to each other.

Michelle breaks the stalemate, bounding toward you. "Come with me," she says.

You want to turn on Diana, tear into her with claws, fists, teeth even. You want drugs, a big fix, and with it, oblivion. You want to jump into a car and feel whatever mix of twisted need and desire the next john tosses your way.

Abuse.

Diana has shattered a very, very fragile thing. And no claws, needles or paid-for sex acts are going to piece it back together. So, for the second time that afternoon you follow, this time with no linking arm.

Diana falls back, still weeping, and Marlene walks with her, Jane bustling along beside, trying to take over, of course.

Samantha walks in the rear and Michelle marches on ahead. You cringe as you remember following her to Jim's so many months ago. Where is she leading you now? She looks great, all shiny head to toe. Hmm.

Beth falls into step beside you. "What happened back there?" she asks, her voice almost too low to hear. "It's him, right? Grimsby."

You appreciate that she leaves off the *Mister*. He doesn't deserve it. But you still want to shut her up. That one word, the *A* word, is as far as you're able to go right now. Now that you've said it, you're not sure you'll ever be able to say it again. You try out a nod, a small one.

She seems to know enough to stay quiet after that. Or maybe she's scared too.

How does she know anyway? How have all these people come together? Jane and Samantha are hangers-on, but the rest of them have only one thing in common. Or two: you. And Grimsby.

It's a bit of a walk Michelle takes you on, and she does so in her typical fashion, out in front, fast.

You see several people you know as you walk down Hastings, then Main, and Cordova. Several double takes, as they try to make sense of your company. There's the Army & Navy store coming up on your left. Great place for cheap boots and clothes. On your right, a series of doors are set back from the street under an overhang. All the way along, people have laid out sleeping bags, even pitched small tents. Collections of stuff are everywhere. The doors are glass, barred. One of them is covered in signs and posters, and that is the door Michelle opens and enters.

You stop at the sight of your own face; it's looking out at you from the poster in the window to the right of the door. Right beside it is a poster of Sarah. Your hand rises from your side to tear down your picture, but the sheet of paper is stuck on the other side of the glass. Your hand falls back, and you gaze at Sarah's face and yours, side by side. She looks a bit like you, Sarah does. You fight off tears and crazy mother-daughter fantasies. Sarah is gone. And she is not your mother.

You look at the pictures some more, and something inside you rises up. You do not want to be a face in a "missing" poster. You do not want to be where Sarah is now. Sarah knew that. She tried to tell you. *Go home*, she said. *They could be me. They could be you.*

You know, deep down inside, that Sarah is dead.

An image flashes into your mind: your heels scrabbling in the gravel while that man tightens his grip on your throat. You never want to be there again. You never, ever want "they" to be you.

You walk through the door and tear your own poster down, leaving Sarah's all alone.

Inside, a woman comes toward you, surprise on her face, as six of you crowd through the door behind Michelle. You look around. Diana's face is a mask. Beth looks bruised, her round cheeks pale, eyes kind of sunken. Marlene stands straight, shoulders back, at the ready. Jane's back is pressed against the door, her expression a mix of fear and disgust.

You see the place through Jane's eyes. It's a drop-in, kind of rundown, but friendly, a basket of condoms on the counter, a battered couch nearby. You've never been here yourself, but you know. It's a place for sex workers. Where they can get help. Your brain hiccups, slots in "you" for "they."

Samantha stands next to Jane, but her face shows only compassion. She has her hand on Jane's arm, and you feel a sob of longing in your throat as you recognize her protectiveness.

"Can I help you?" a voice says, and you turn to see the startled woman who stands now at the top of the three steps that lead up from the entry area.

Michelle is striding up those steps, and you see the recognition. "Raven," Michelle says, and Raven bursts into a grin.

Raven is black, much blacker than you, and elegant and strong and beautiful. You like her instantly. "Michelle! You look great!" she says. And they embrace.

An outreach worker, you guess. Your knees buckle slightly, and a hand grasps your elbow—Beth's. She gestures with her head, and together the two of you step forward and climb the stairs.

There are so many people to be managed, you realize, and at the same time there is something dreadful to track down and force out into the open. Your sickness is rising.

"I want to call my mother," Jane says suddenly, interrupting whatever Michelle is saying to Raven.

Another woman has joined them from a backroom and she whisks Jane off, presumably to help her do that.

You see your own fear mirrored on Diana's face. "No mothers," she says.

And you agree, ill at the thought of your mother's eyes on you, her feelings looping through you, tangling everything even tighter than it already is. You're not ready for that. Yet. Having Beth here is hard enough.

"Michelle," you say suddenly, your voice sharp. "Jane can't tell about us."

Michelle abandons Raven, goes off in search of Jane, who is probably already weeping on the phone, begging her mother for a ride, probably telling her everything in one big rush.

Raven turns to the five of you who are left. "Let's sit down," she says. She ushers you into a room with a big round table, and fetches apple juice while you arrange yourselves.

You gulp the juice, your body screaming for sugar—and something stronger. You probably have half an hour of sanity left before you start shaking and vomiting.

Raven is looking at you; she knows exactly where you're at. You can see it. You find that you trust it.

"Now, tell me why you're here," she says quietly as she closes the door. She addresses no one in particular, avoids eye contact.

You are surprised, but grateful, when Marlene speaks first.

"It's my grandpa," she says. "I think he hurt them." She pauses, as if it takes great effort to spit out the next word, the more precise one. Finally, "Abused them," she says. "Kaya and Diana."

Samantha has her hand on Beth's arm, but Beth seems oblivious to her. All her attention is fixed on you. You hold her gaze for a long moment after Marlene falls silent.

Speak, her eyes say. *Tell.*

You turn back to Raven.

"Yes," you say at last. "Her grandfather. Mr. Grimsby. He abused us."

They feel like the biggest words ever spoken. They are certainly the biggest words ever spoken by you. And with them said, you find, you are done. You can say no more.

Raven sees it immediately, the nausea taking over, your addiction demanding its next meal. She moves you to a couch, where she can talk just to you, and she tells you that you need a bed, that you need to go into a treatment centre today.

"There's no point," she says, "to stretching this out. You need to get off the drugs so you can deal with the abuse. Your best chance is now." She pauses, as if considering. Then, "You've seen the posters. You know what's happening to women down here."

You think of Sarah on the swings, Sarah lighting the candle in front of the stone. *They could be me. They could be you.*

You nod, ever so slightly.

"What's that?" Raven says.

"All right," you whisper.

Δ

Beth calls Mom after that and she comes. And she cries and so do you. You're pretty sick, by then.

Raven will take you to the detox centre herself, she says. And you run to the toilet to throw up one more time before you go.

Calling Mom that night is rough: getting up the nerve, waiting while it rings. She's brisk on the phone. "Tell me where you are. I'll be right there."

I wait for her on that couch by the door, while Kaya stays in back with Diana and Michelle. Jane's mother sweeps Jane and Samantha away in the meantime. Turns out Jane got her call in before Michelle had a chance to stop her.

Mom arrives strong, but there's something about her shoulders and her cheeks, as if the bones in her back and her face have melted a bit and sunken down. She hugs me and holds me away from her and looks into my face.

"You're all right," she says, and I bite my tongue on a wailed *No, I'm not. I'm not.* She doesn't need that right now.

"Where is she?" she says.

Raven brings Kaya out then, and Mom wraps her arms around Kaya without a word and without looking into her face like she did into mine. It's like she doesn't want to see what's there. Not yet. She just wants to hold her messed-up daughter in her arms.

"I'm taking her to treatment tonight," Raven says to Mom. "I've found her a bed." She hesitates. "If that's all right with you."

Mom nods, still holding my sister tight.

In the end, Kaya has to wriggle herself free. "I've got to go, Mom," she says.

So we go home without her, yet again. And despite the fact that Marlene and Michelle are in the back seat of the car, Mom cries all the way. Tears drip off her chin. At the red lights, the sobs turn to wails.

I watch the tears, the scrunched-up face, and wonder about the big cold space inside my chest. When I'm alone in my room . . . I think to myself. When I'm alone I'll cry.

CHAPTER FIFTEEN

Kaya

You stand in the grungy little bathroom and splash cold water on your face, doing your best to keep your eyes off the tiny mirror above the sink. Your makeup is gone. One whole side of your face is black and blue. Your side aches from throwing up with bruised ribs.

And you remember.

Δ

You first found out about Mr. Grimsby one day when you were playing in the ravine with Diana. You were in Grade Three then, and it was early in the year. Diana kept stopping that day, like she needed to be somewhere else. The two of you had blocked a tiny creek and a pond was forming. You were looking for something to serve as a boat. And you looked up and Diana was still.

"What are you doing? Help me find a piece of wood that will float properly," you said.

"I . . . I have to go," Diana replied.

"You have to go where?" That's when she told you. She wasn't ashamed yet, so the story came out easily. He had just moved in on the street behind hers, stepped across the lane and introduced himself, a cane in his hand and a hat on his head.

"And he did a handstand, right in our backyard, even though he's old!" Diana said, lingering on the word *old*. "He invited us to visit, me and my sisters, and I went. All by myself." She sounded proud of herself at this point: she, the youngest. "He served real tea, in china cups. And the prettiest little cookies. His friend made them. Jennifer. His housekeeper, I think she is. And you should see inside his house. Lots of kids play there. They do projects and things. Outside too. He has this toy car you can actually drive. But he invited me in for tea! He doesn't do that for everybody."

You wondered about the story a little bit. Going into the house. "Isn't that dangerous?" you asked. "Going into his house alone, I mean."

"Oh, it's not alone. Jennifer's there. And besides, Mom and Dad met him. Remember?"

"Right." You had to admit, it sounded fun. Not so much the tea and cookies, but the toy car. And the handstand. You loved doing gymnastics, but you hadn't mastered the handstand yet and you had never seen a grown man do one except on TV.

Diana left that day, and you stayed and found just the right bit of wood, and launched it on the pond, but it wasn't much fun, really, after all that. And you soon felt wet and cold.

When you arrived home, you turned the door handle and pushed, letting the door open slowly, silently. If you could just sneak into your room, wet and muddy as you were, you could relax for a bit. Draw maybe. Or write, even.

The house seemed quiet at first, and you put a foot on the bottom step. Your room was right at the top. Then, there was Mom in the front hall, hair kind of wild, eyes flashing.

"You're filthy. Where have you been?" She was like that sometimes, on top of you out of the blue. Furious. Just as often, it took no effort to sneak past her to the safety of your room. You had no idea why. You didn't know then that Dad was sick.

"In the ravine," you responded, "with Diana." Mom didn't need to know that Diana had gone away and you stayed there all alone.

Δ

The day you went to Mr. G's with Diana, it was because of rain, and also because of the box. She had come to the ravine unwillingly, because you had wheedled. You were making a sort of a house now, with rooms, up on a flat place above the creek, under a tree. No, not a house, you told your friend. "A fort. That's the river, rushing by. Many have drowned there. And here is the fort, well guarded."

Diana got into it a bit, finding pieces of wood to make the walls, assigning areas for sleeping, for cooking, for eating. But then it started to rain. At first it didn't make it through the trees, but soon drips were finding their way down the neck of your shirt.

She stopped and looked at you. A serious look.

"What?" you said, putting down the piece of the south wall that you had been wrestling into place.

"Today you should come," she said.

"Come where?" You knew perfectly well.

"To see him. Look. Look what he gave me."

Diana held out her hand, and you stepped forward, and breathed a long breath of wonder, lifting your fingers to touch. She was holding a tiny golden box, painted with the most delicate, astonishing scene you had ever seen. A swan glided across smooth water, leaving a long triangular wake. Over and under the swan a willow tree grew and reflected, and on the sloping shore beneath the tree, a girl sat in a white dress, knees drawn up, arms circling them, entranced by the same vision that was entrancing you.

With two fingers, Diana pressed on the edge of the lid, and the scene was broken as the box opened, revealing its blue velvet lining, fat and inviting.

She looked up at you, smiling. "I'm going to keep my best necklace inside," she said. "He gave it to me. It's mine." And, "I told him all about you, and he officially invited you. Officially," she repeated.

A tree branch shifted under the rain's weight and a small torrent fell right on your head. You swiped at your face with a dirty hand as Diana clicked the lid down and whisked the box to the safety of her pocket.

"All right," you said. "I'll come."

Δ

His first words to the pair of you were "What a pair of raga-muffins!" His accent was funny, precise. Snooty, you might have called it. He had white hair and a soft, clean-shaven face, with big pale eyes. His smile was full of warmth and humour, despite the snooty accent. His teeth were big and white and straight. He was so old, they were probably fake, you thought. *Ragamuffins* might sound like an insult, but it didn't feel like one. It felt as if he loved nothing better than to welcome a pair of damp, muddy girls into his neat-and-tidy house.

Diana beamed up at him. "Mr. Grimsby, this is Kaya," she said. Then she turned her beaming face on you. "Kaya, this is Mr. Grimsby. I told you he wouldn't mind that we're all muddy. You don't, do you, Mr. Grimsby?"

His smile widened. "Not at all. Lovely to meet you, Kaya. We'll get the two of you cleaned up straightaway. Please leave your shoes by the door, and hang your coats on those hooks."

It turned out that everything Diana had told you was true. After you cleaned up in the guest bathroom, with pretty embroidered guest washcloths and towels, Mr. Grimsby poured out tea from a silver pot into tiny china cups. He served homemade cookies.

He bustled in and out of the kitchen, looking very proper, you thought. His shirt had long sleeves and a collar, and kind of a crisp look to it. His pants were crisp too, and his shoes had laces and gleamed. He wore reading glasses on a string around his neck. His hair was long and wispy, not neat like all the rest of him.

"Can I show Kaya the toys now?" Diana asked when you had barely swallowed the last bite of your first cookie. "And the other boxes?"

She showed you toys unlike any you had ever seen, let alone been free to play with. But best of all was the man himself. He asked questions and listened to the answers, his head cocked just a bit. He wanted to know about Mom and Dad and Beth. He wanted to know about Grade Three, about your teacher, about other students. He wanted to know about your passions. He was fascinated by your tales of what you and Diana were creating in the ravine.

Diana bubbled over with excitement, showing you paintings and dolls and a dollhouse filled with tiny perfect furniture and quilts on the beds, instructing you to tell him about this and him to tell you about that. She told her own stories as well, and answered his questions about things that had happened since her last visit.

After a bit, Mr. Grimsby stopped asking questions and smiling at everything you said. He asked you to set the dollhouse straight, and then he told you that it was time to go home. Just you. "Diana has a bit of tidying to do from last time she was here," he said quietly. "You take yourself off now, dear, but do feel free to come for another visit soon!"

You were surprised to find yourself walking down the sidewalk all alone, surprised and kind of deflated, empty inside. At home, Dad was in bed. One of his bad days. And nobody even asked you where you had been. Not that you had any intention of telling. You were pretty sure what that would lead to: *No, no and no.*

You planned to keep Mr. G all to yourself, and a whole week passed before you had a chance to go back.

He was in his front garden, pulling weeds and pruning roses. "Good morning, Kaya," he said when you got his attention. He smiled up at you and then you saw him see your face, really see it. He struggled to his feet. "What's wrong, my dear?"

Your face dissolved then. You hated the feel of it. The wobbling chin, the squinching cheeks and eyes. You knew just what it looked like, how pathetic it was. Mom had always huffed her impatience when your face did those things.

Mr. Grimsby didn't huff. He invited you in. He got you to sit in one of the big fancy chairs at the dining table with a little stool for your feet so you would be comfortable. He made tea, and gave it to you in a flowered cup edged in gold with lots of milk and sugar stirred in. Then he asked you all about it. You talked and talked and he looked at you and listened and his eyes even filled up with tears when you told about how sick your dad was. How Mom had told you, finally, that he had cancer.

He poured you another cup of tea, even sweeter than the last. He asked you more questions, and while you were answering, he pulled a pad of paper in front of him and picked up a thick pencil, and he started to draw.

You were puzzled, and you stopped talking.

He looked up and saw you staring at the paper. His lips tensed slightly. "It's all right, Kaya. I'm just going to draw while we chat." He looked at you and his face relaxed into a smile. "I'm drawing you, actually. See?"

And he turned the paper toward you, and you looked at the simple outline of head and shoulders.

"Now, you were telling me about that fort of yours. It's mostly gone now, you say?"

It was hard to keep talking while he was so intent on

the pencil in his hand, but whenever you paused, he asked another question, and eventually he put the paper down and turned his attention full on you once again, and you talked and talked and talked.

At one point he got up and went in search of something. When he came back, he pressed a tiny metal swan into your hand. "It's pewter," he said. It was a dark silvery colour, not white like a real swan, but it had all a real swan's grace and beauty, and the tiny size to make it extra special.

"A swan," you breathed, "like in the picture on Diana's box." It wasn't quite as special as Diana's box, but you pushed that thought away, ran your finger down the slope of the creature's back.

"Swans are special," he said, "just like you. You can keep it in your pocket. For comfort." He crouched down and placed a hand on each of your upper arms. "Our little secret." Then he looked at his watch. "Now, my dear, I think it's time for you to go home. Or your mother will wonder where you've been."

As you got up and walked toward the door, fingering the swan in your pocket, you glanced at the pad of paper on the table, longing to see what he had drawn, but he had flipped another page over top, and it didn't seem polite to ask.

Off you went, home.

"Is that you, Kaya?" Mom called from the kitchen.

"Yes," you said, your voice coming out as a squeak. You drew a breath. "Yes," you called out, more forcefully.

"I don't like you going off like that, without a word to anyone," Mom continued, not setting foot outside the kitchen.

"Sorry, Mom," you called back. "I'm going upstairs."

And up you went, to your messy room, where you curled up in your safe, warm bed, put the tiny swan beside you on the pillow and thought and thought and thought.

Δ

It wasn't long before you went back. And it was just as special as before. And like the other times, the moment came when he said that it was time to go. "I hope to see you again soon," he said, and his smile reached right inside you. He wanted to see you! "And next time you come . . . which I hope will be soon . . . I'd like you to come to the sliding door there. See?"

He was pointing to the sliding door in the dining room. "You can come in from the lane and up onto the deck, and try the door. If it's locked, I'm not home or I'm busy. If it's open, you can just come right in!" His grin was broad and welcoming as he led you out onto the deck and pointed to the gap in the hedge that separated the garden from the lane.

A crackly feeling way down at the bottom of your spine sounded a warning. But it could not compete with the warmth, or even with the secrets themselves, which felt special, just for you.

Tomorrow, you were thinking, as you half galloped home. You'd come back tomorrow.

Δ

And you did. Tomorrow and tomorrow and tomorrow. Week after week. Month after month. Sometimes the sliding door was locked, and you wandered off, the tight ball of anticipation and fear that had gathered in your gut gradually crumbling, spreading thick poison everywhere. Sometimes he went away. Sometimes the door was locked but you would hear a hubbub from the front. You'd go round by the street and join the kids in the big toy cars.

One of those times, Diana was there, shrieking with laughter as she barrelled down the sidewalk in a go-kart. When she saw you, all her laughter drained away, and she left quickly.

Often, though, the door would slide open at your touch, your gut would clench as you entered. And he would be there. And he would smile and rise from his desk or the kitchen table or the big easy chair in front of the fireplace. Always, he would make you tea or juice and offer cookies. Always, you would sit and talk, and he would listen.

Sometimes the moment would come and he would say, "Time to go now." And you would. Other times, he would glance at the basement stairs. And you would descend. Step. Step. Step. And you would go into that room. And, as best you could, you would do what Mr. G wanted. Over the years, he wanted more and more things. It was your job, you told yourself. He was kind to you. He listened. And he asked of you these . . . things. They were the least you could do. You prided yourself a little bit on your strength.

When you were upstairs, he never spoke of what happened in that room. The only connection between upstairs and down was the drawings. He liked to draw upstairs. And he liked to show you his drawings upstairs. The drawings of other children. Children from his trips. Children with no clothes. They looked happy in his drawings and glowed, like angels. And you told yourself that they were happy. And that you should be happy too.

Δ

You had been visiting Mr. Grimsby for years when Dad died, so it was natural to visit him, to tell him about it, and it was a relief to get out of the house, away from Mom, who went kind of manic, and Beth, who shut herself away in her room. Through the closed door, you could almost hear her munching away on cookies or something.

The morning after he died, you opened the front door and slipped out of the house. First, you tried the ravine. You had not been there in years, not since Grade Three. The fort was all gone, but the tree was still there. You squeezed yourself into its low-down bend, and swung your heels, scuffing at the dry dirt.

Harder and harder you swung them, smashing your feet into the stump, feeling the force in your legs, the solidity of the tree. For a moment—only one—you thought about going to see if Diana was home, but the two of you had grown apart long ago. You didn't really talk to each other anymore. In the end, you freed yourself from the tree, dusted yourself off and set off to visit Mr. G. And he sat you down, gave you a sandwich and a glass of milk, and listened, really listened. He even got tears in his eyes just like that first time years before. And he never once glanced at the basement stairs.

Δ

He came to the funeral, with Jennifer. And sent you home later with those beautiful orange roses that Beth caught you with on the stairs.

After that, though, the sliding door was locked a lot of the time. And even when it wasn't, Mr. Grimsby said "Time to go now" much more often. He hardly ever led you to the basement stairs, he listened to you with less attention and he snapped at you more. The locked door, the *Time to go*'s, the darting eyes, the nasty comments, all of that wounded, and you found yourself hoping for the one thing that told you that he wanted you, the basement. And that made you sick. That meant that you *were* sick. And the secret grew more and more unwieldy; it pushed at you; it threatened you; it spoke cruel words to you. *Pervert*, it called you. *Slut*.

The innocence of mothers and sisters and friends revolted you. Only the innocence of animals would do. You would come home from that locked door and walk into your house and fall to your knees as Sybilla bounded up to you. She filled your arms. Her fur enveloped your face. You breathed in dog. And—when you could find her—cat.

Δ

You were almost thirteen, just finishing Grade Seven, when it ended for good.

You were only eleven and a half when you first got your period, but you never mentioned that to Mr. G. It was personal, awkward and, well, kind of gross, so even though you told Mr. G absolutely everything else, and loved how he questioned you, drawing you out and listening to every word, you left out that one development and never went to his house when you had it.

Until one time.

It was only a few days until your birthday, and as always, Mr. G asked you what you would like for a gift and what kind of cake you wanted.

Every year, you had asked for art supplies, which you kept at his house so the two of you could draw and paint together. He was gradually teaching you everything he knew. And you always picked a white cake with chocolate frosting, and Jennifer baked it.

This year you asked for a new angle brush and a tube of cerulean acrylic paint (your favourite blue). You sipped tea, ate two cookies. And as always, you watched his face for clues as to what was going to happen next. And that day, for the first time in months, he directed you toward the basement door. What you did not know was that your body was in the process of betraying you. Your period, which you had kept hidden for more than a year, was starting even as you walked down those stairs.

Five minutes later, he was flinging you to the floor and shouting, "Filthy little whore!"

He was gone from the room before you had even taken in what had happened. Bruised and humiliated, you straightened your skirt and fled up the stairs, taking in as you did so that he was at the basement sink, scrubbing his hand and arm as if he had just been subjected to radiation.

As you walked home, your belly squirming with a nasty mix of shame and cramps, you thought that you would never go back.

Your birthday passed. You were pretty sure that no art supplies had been purchased, no cake baked. Anyway, for five days you still had your period, and those three words echoed in your head, *Filthy little whore.*

But more days passed, and your teachers were unfair, Mom snapped at you, Beth ignored you and Michelle was never there. You longed for Mr. G's listening ear. Besides, what had happened must have been a terrible mistake. He must have thought you did that on purpose, went there with your period. Maybe there was a way that you could apologize—kind of explain without really spelling it out.

Two weeks later, you went back.

Δ

You slipped through the narrow gap in the hedge off the lane as always. That day, you hesitated near the hedge, gazed at the tidy backyard and reflected on what an odd way this was to approach a person's house. A sneaky way.

You felt your brow furrow, the skin over your cheekbones stiffen. This space—the gap in the thick hedge (that you now had to turn sideways to pass through), the raised gardens, the pebbled paths and the expanse of cement under the deck—had always troubled you. You had always had to force yourself to pass through the hedge, to cross the yard, to climb the wooden steps to the deck, to place your hand on the metal handle, to slide the door open, to push the curtain out of the way and step inside.

You had never liked it, but you had never questioned it either. This was the way Mr. G had told you to come to his house, so this was the way you came. But now, everything had changed.

The day before, you had walked along Fourteenth Avenue, nonchalant as could be, and seen that his car was parked right in front, that the curtains were open, so you knew he was still there. He only went away in the fall anyway, but you had wondered if after what had happened, he might go. Seeing his car and the open curtains reassured you that maybe it was all right.

Now, for the very first time in, what—five years?—you decided that if that door did not slide open for you, you were going to knock on it. So, you paused. You smoothed down your skirt. Then you squared your shoulders and you walked. Along one of the pebbled paths, up the wooden steps, across the deck shaded by the neighbours' massive beech tree, its leaves changing colour.

Mr. G always complained about that tree, the shade it created, the mess when the leaves fell. More than once he had lopped off branches, and been indignant for weeks when the tree's owners called the city.

"Branches hanging over my property are my property," he would say, and you would nod and wait for the conversation to shift to something more interesting. You thought the tree was beautiful, and especially in early fall.

Heat pulsed through your chest as you reached out your hand to try the door. Locked. The heat pulsed again, radiating into your limbs, your throat. You pressed the side of your face against the door and listened, but you could not hear a sound. You raised your hand to knock, hesitated, and let it drop.

The window that looked into the kitchen above the sink was small, and high up, but you should be able to see in if you gripped the ledge with your fingers and pulled yourself up on your toes. On tiptoe, you made your way along the side of the house. Still on tiptoe, you grasped that ledge, and you looked. All that heat whooshed through you, top to bottom, almost sending you into a heap on the ground. He was there, sitting at the kitchen table. He was angled away from you, but you could see precisely what he was doing. He had a small easel set up on the kitchen table, a photo clipped to the top of it. You couldn't see what was in the photo, but you could see the drawing, at least enough to get the idea. You'd seen plenty of his drawings before, after all. He was drawing the torso of a child. A girl, perhaps nine or ten years old. Naked.

You might have knocked then, or made any sound at all, and he would have looked. He would have come to the door and spoken words to you. You were pretty sure you would not have liked those words. You knew then, in that moment, what you had never allowed yourself to know over the course of the last year or more, when the door had been locked so often, when the visits had grown shorter.

You knew in that moment that Mr. G didn't want you anymore. Mr. G had not wanted you in a long, long time.

So you let go of the ledge and settled back onto the flats of your feet and crept away, down the steps, along the pebble path. You took more care not to be seen slipping through the hedge into the lane than you ever had before. And the shame that filled you up was like vomit and liquid shit: it shot through your veins, reaching into your toes, your fingertips, your earlobes, oozing out of your pores; it filled your guts, backing up into your mouth and your nose. You felt it at the roots of your hair, in the beds of your nails. The tears that appeared on your face stank of it.

Most of all, you felt it in your crotch, your butt, your chest, all the places that were changing, hairs poking their way out through your skin where no hairs should be, fat gathering, shaping your body in ways that could not be hidden no matter how hard you tried to flatten yourself out and squeeze into the little-girl dresses that Mr. G liked so much.

Δ

There it is now. All of it, playing through your head, while all around you people *know*. No protection. No filter. Not even any privacy. You ease open the bathroom door and peer out toward the exit.

"Ready to go?" Raven asks.

You jump. Of course she'd be right there waiting. In her strong loving presence, your resistance slips away. For now.

CHAPTER SIXTEEN

Kaya

Detox is not worth writing about. Neither is treatment. You do everything, jump through all the hoops, obey all the rules. Except for one. You will not talk about Grimsby. You will not explain. Everyone else does. In group everyone tells their stories, everyone explains their troubles, the horrors that led them to the street, the beatings, the rapes, the neglect. And you listen and listen and listen. You tell yourself that if you hear one story like yours, just one, you'll open up your mouth and tell.

But you don't. You *do not*.

Your lips stay sealed. You concentrate on that seal, on the slight pressure of lip on lip, easy enough to break to drink, to eat, even, sometimes, to breathe. And it's not as if you never speak. But not in group. Never in group.

In the end, they let you go home anyway. Mom and Beth pick you up, and try to chat with you on the drive, but you can only mumble in response. Their discomfort fills the car, and you wish, you wish for . . . Who? Your mind casts about for someone, anyone, to wish for. You come up with a single name, and it's on a poster downtown. That person is gone. You know in your heart she is dead. And she couldn't help you anyway. All she could say was *Go home*, which is precisely what you are doing right now.

Why does it have to be so hard?

In your head, thousands and thousands of times each day, the refrain repeats: *You can always go back. They can't make you stay. You can always, always go back.*

Beth

At home, I grab Kaya's suitcase, recovered somehow and probably full of vermin, from the car and carry it straight up the stairs. Kaya follows and Mom takes up the rear. I feel hope and fear well up.

"I hope you like what we did," Mom says, filling the stair-well with chatter. "We cleaned up, and we painted too. We thought you should have a fresh start."

I turn quickly in the bedroom, eager to catch Kaya's face when she sees the warm colours, the brand new duvet cover, the cozy rug, the collection of framed photos. Mom and I worked hard on it for three weekends. Michelle and Diana helped for an afternoon. Jane and Samantha for another. Even Marlene came by, dropped off by her dad.

We used the photos to show the parts of Kaya's life that were joyful, and the other stuff to create something fresh and new.

It's been a strange journey, the last thirty days. I put

everything into getting Kaya home, but the minute she entered treatment, it felt as if my job was over. I helped paint and decorate this room, sure, but everything hinges now on Kaya, on her recovery, on her staying power. I feel kind of empty a lot of the time. Empty and scared. If she relapses—I know we're not supposed to say *fails*—what will that mean for me? I find myself wanting to scream that out a lot these days: *What about me?*

I guess I'm taking it one day at a time too. And I'm going without the ice cream. I do have my own project, on the side. And school, of course.

Anyway, just now, Kaya stands in that fresh, clean room, arms at her sides. Her smile is small, but it's there. "Thanks, you guys," she says.

Kaya

"Thanks, you guys," you say. You even manage to smile at them. They are being kind. You know that. But you kind of wanted to crawl back into your nest, to snug down in the heap of bedding, or in the tangle of your old clothes.

You smile and smile until they go, until they leave you to settle yourself, but when they are gone, you are too exhausted to begin.

Δ

The next day, Mom comes into your room without knocking and sits right down on your bed. "I'm going to work," she says, "but Beth is staying home with you. She's got permission to miss two whole weeks."

You grunt and roll over, but Mom's not done. "Your alarm's set for eight, honey," she says. "Remember, no sleeping the days away. And Beth will walk you to your meeting this afternoon."

Your grunt's a groan this time. Mom squeezes your shoulder through the duvet, and then leaves. You don't plan to sleep the day away, but on your first morning back in your own room, you'd like to be free to relax. In your last moment of consciousness, you reach out and turn off the alarm. Sleep takes you away.

You're furious when another hand grasps your shoulder, when a perky voice calls out, "Wake up, Kaya. Wake up! It's ten past eight."

It's pretty gutsy of her; you'll give her that. But it makes you mad just the same. You roll onto your back, wrenching your shoulder from Beth's grasp. "I know what time it is, all right? Can't you see I'm sleeping?"

You hear Beth breathe in courage. "You have to get up, Kaya. You're not allowed to sleep past eight. Remember?"

Your eyes are open now, your elbows pulled under you, propping you up. "And what business is that of yours?"

"I'm your helper. Remember? I have to get you up."

You glare.

"And besides, everybody's coming over."

Your lower jaw falls. "What? Who?"

"You'll see. Now, get up!" She smiles slightly and her brow quirks. "Or should I send them up here?"

That does it. You are up.

You take your time, though, getting ready, going through the clothes in your closet, each item so familiar yet so strange. You're not sure you can bear to put these clothes on; the girl who once wore them does not exist anymore.

You see it then, and stop. Slightly crooked on the hanger, badly wrinkled and obviously well worn, the summer dress— the little girl's dress—its splashy pattern still bright, its skirt still full. More than a year ago, you crumpled that dress into the back corner of your closet, shoved it behind heaps of clothes and other junk. Away.

Now, it has returned.

You drop your hands to your knees and double over.

Mr. G liked that dress. It was his favourite, actually, so you wore it a lot back then. It's sleeveless with a high neck and a full skirt, covered in oversized flowers. Mr. Grimsby said they were roses, but you could never see how he knew that. They were just big blobs of colour, really.

Anyway, he liked it, so you wore it. You wore it down those basement steps quite a few times, and Mr. G always took special care with it, which was not true with all your clothes. It was tight across the chest and through the shoulders that last summer, and your knees stuck out the bottom, but you kept squeezing yourself into it.

"What are you wearing that old thing for?" Mom said once. "It's a little girl's dress, not a teenager's."

She had jumped at the venom in your response. How you hated those words: *little girl*. And, even worse, *teenager*.

You can still remember the feel of the cotton skirt

clutched in your hands as you turned away from the kitchen window that day, after watching Mr. G draw one of his naked pictures. Now, as you wait for the nausea to pass, you take in for the first time that the children in those photographs, those drawings—the little girls from faraway countries that Mr. Grimsby so loved to draw—are real. Suddenly you really get it.

You get that he did it to them too, that he made them do things, that he hurt them. That he was kind to them and made them trust him and then he betrayed them.

And you realize that there must be other girls right here. Maybe there was even another girl after you, an eight- or nine-year-old who's out there right now, hurt and confused and scared.

The nausea is not going to pass. You sink to your knees. It's probably never going to pass—

"What are you doing?"

You start, which results in a sort of tumble sideways off your knees and onto your butt. You scramble to your feet and find yourself fact to face with the monster's grand-daughter. Marlene.

"Hey," she says. "Are you all right?"

"I'm fine," you say. "Did you just walk into my room?"

"I knocked," she says, "but nobody answered. And you're supposed to be downstairs."

"I don't even know you," you say.

She harrumphs or grunts or some strange thing. "Listen," she says. "I have to tell you something. My mom wouldn't let me near Grandpa, not after I was six. I never understood why. I loved visiting him . . . All those toys and things. He was so much fun. And then one day, no more visits. I kind of remember her and Dad yelling about it. But she would not change her mind. After that, I only ever saw him at big family parties. And she kept a close eye on me."

You back your way up to your bed as you listen, and plunk down into a sitting position. Stare. She stands stiff as she talks, taking a deep breath at the end of every sentence. She sort of runs out of steam at one point, and you wait, ready now to see it through. Ready now to hear.

"Well, since I saw you outside the church, I've been thinking and thinking, and I realized that I remember something." Her face is stony now, like she doesn't want to say it. "It was a bath. I was six, I guess, and he got me to help in the garden, and I was all muddy and he gave me a bath. I don't think it felt weird to me, really, though I know now it was. But then Mom showed up at the house. She charged into the bathroom and took over. I was still kind of muddy, but she whisked me out of that tub and into my clothes and out of that house. I was crying because she was in such a hurry that she was kind of rough, and I didn't understand."

You look up at her, understanding very well. Too well.

"And that was the last time I ever went to Grandpa's house," she says.

You're not sure what to do with yourself when she falls silent, and neither is she. After a minute, you say, "I need to get dressed. I'll see you down there, okay?"

She nods. Her feet make hollow clumping noises on the stairs.

Δ

It takes you a minute to move. Then you rise off the bed and yank on a pair of stretchy pants, pull a T-shirt over your head, go to your closet again, rip that dress off the hanger and head downstairs.

They're all sitting around in the living room, and they look like a bunch of startled rabbits when you walk in. All six pairs of eyes jump to the clutch of fabric in your hand.

You stand there, at a full stop.

"What have you got that for?" Beth asks. "That dress is way too small for you."

You feel your body sway, tears coming up from way down deep. Scary tears.

Diana stands. "I think she wore it to see him," she says.

Beth marches up to you then, blazing with fury. She grabs the dress out of your hand, walks straight to the fireplace and tosses it onto the heap of ash. "We need to destroy this," she says.

Nobody questions her, not even you. You watch them rushing around as if a little fire could erase everything that has happened to you. You want to reach inside all their grey wrinkly brains and snatch up their nasty thoughts and burn them instead of the dress. They mustn't think about *that*. But they are. That's why they're here. That's why Beth rushes off to the basement to find kerosene or some other flammable liquid. That's why Michelle is rooting around on the mantel looking for one of those long lighters or some extra-long matches, so that no one lights herself on fire along with the dress. That's why Marlene and Diana and Samantha and Jane are making a neat semicircle of dining room chairs around the fireplace.

A ritual is taking shape. And it is all because they know about *that*.

Beth emerges from the basement with a dusty bottle of something called methyl hydrate. For fondue, she says. She douses the dress with it. Michelle holds the lighter out to you. You back away from her.

Marlene steps forward. "We'll light it together," she says, "all three of us." She means her and Diana and you. The three "victims" in the room. Diana is trembling a bit too, but she steps forward, places her hand over Marlene's.

You shake your head violently and drop onto a chair. "Go ahead," you manage to say in a scratchy whisper. "I'll just watch."

Marlene and Diana press the button and the flame that shoots from the lighter senses the flammable liquid before it quite reaches the fabric, whooshes and envelops the heap of dress. You think of ants swarming over a carcass. Marlene and Diana sit down and all of you watch the fire consume the dress.

After a while you are staring at a crinkly, smoking mess. It smells bad. You look around the room and see all eyes, six pairs, on you. You shove yourself to your feet and turn away.

Beth

I'm confused when I see what Kaya is holding in her hand. It's so familiar, that dress. Kaya wore it and wore it, long after she had grown out of it. Mom told her to stop, but never went so far as to take the dress away. I am the one who found it wadded up in the back of the closet, smoothed out the wrinkles and put it on a hanger. I imagined how pleased Kaya would be to see it again, even though she definitely wouldn't be able to squeeze into it now.

When Kaya starts to cry, though, and Diana says what she does, I hardly know what I'm doing until I'm standing in front of the fireplace with the methyl hydrate.

Now, the thing is done.

Jane says, "I'm going to make tea," and heads for the kitchen as if this were a grown-ups' bridge party.

Samantha meets my eyes, and somehow I know what to do, how to pull us all back from the brink. At least, I know how to try.

I feel a warm, strong place in my gut and send the words straight out from there. "Let's go into the dining room," I say. "Bring your chairs."

They look kind of startled, but seem willing enough to pick up their chairs and follow me. Jane arrives from the kitchen with a tray of cups and spoons.

I dash up to my room and fetch my "magic boxes." No time to think about the fact that no human outside my family has seen me perform a trick since I was eight years old, no time to take in how crazy it is to offer up a deck of cards in a house that still smells of a little girl's dress burned to ash.

When I get back, we rearrange the room: the table against one wall, the chairs out for an audience of six. On the table I un-stack the two boxes, pull out my trusty deck of cards, several large scarves and my favourite stuffed animal, a small pink rabbit with long silky ears.

Jane serves tea. Kaya sits off-centre, flanked by Michelle

and Diana. Her hands are clasped in her lap, and she looks at me as if the contents of her head and heart went up the chimney along with the smoke. Samantha sits behind her, beaming that kindness of hers to all of us.

And me, I put on a show. I manage the card tricks all right. And get a small rush of pleasure when Kaya agrees to pull a card from the deck.

"Is it the nine of spades?" I ask soon after, and Kaya grins. She actually grins.

"Yes!" she says as she brandishes the card.

Maybe she remembers how I screwed up the same trick so many years before. Whether she does or not, I see gladness in her eyes today.

But the rabbit and the boxes, I just don't have it down. Patter, yes. I have them all rocking in their chairs with laughter. But when it comes to the transfer, I lose my nerve. I know they will see. And I am not about to commit the ultimate sin of magician-ship: revealing the trick. So, I go with a rabbit that will not budge, a rabbit that has no wish to be part of a magic show.

In the end, the rabbit seeks solace in Kaya's arms. And I gulp as Kaya clasps the small creature to her chest.

Kaya

They can't all take two weeks off school, but every one of them stops in every single day, sometimes singly, sometimes in pairs or threes, sometimes in the late afternoon, sometimes at night.

Every day, Beth walks you to the three o'clock meeting in a nearby church basement, and returns ninety minutes later to walk you home. The meetings get you down. Nobody there is really like you. No kids, for a start. And nobody has lived downtown. Plus, you're pretty sure that nobody has ever traded sex for a fix. They all sit in their living rooms, comfy as anything, and drink good scotch . . . At least that's what you believe for the first few days.

You do get up and talk once, since it is so clearly expected. You say the required words: "Hi. My name is Kaya and I'm an addict." But you're not about to tell these West Side folks about turning tricks on the Downtown Eastside, or about heroin, or about what that man did to you three blocks away from this very church. You're not about to tell them any of that.

On the first Thursday, Mom takes the afternoon off from work so that she can drive you downtown to meet with Raven, just the two of you. You've been looking forward to it all week, a chance to feel truly, completely understood and at home. But Raven sits back in her chair, watches and listens as you talk and talk. Her face remains clear as you tell her about those rich-people meetings, how nobody there could possibly understand you. She offers no mm-hmms, no nods of understanding. All she says once she's listened for a bit is "How do you know? Did you try?"

You whine on a bit more after that, but the word *bluster* comes to mind, the realization overwhelming you. You can see in Raven's face that she is simply letting you wind down like one of those old-fashioned toys, a key slowly revolving in its back.

At the end she hugs you, looks into your eyes and says, "You're doing great, Kaya. Keep it up." When you ask if you can come see her again the next week, she pauses. Then she shakes her head. "I don't think so," she says. "Down the road, sure, if you still want to, but for now, stick with the program. It's a good one."

Mom is right outside in the car. She drives you straight to your meeting. "Beth will be here to pick you up after," she says, giving you her version of a hug.

You give a small squeeze back. You like Raven's style of hugging better, but at least Mom is trying.

In the meeting you look around. What would Raven see? You have no idea, but this time when you look, you see how crumpled some of the people look, and not just their clothes or uncombed hair or smudged makeup, but them. Several look as if they have been crying for weeks, and one looks as if she'll soon have her fingers gnawed down to the knuckle. Despite this, you see them chatting with one another, reaching out. As you look around the room, three people meet your eyes and make the effort to smile at you. You cast your mind back over the past four days and remember the stories. You glossed over them then, but now you replay them for yourself. You remember the friendliness. And you remember how you have snubbed every single person who tried to talk to you. But still they smile.

You straighten in your chair. You mentally place Raven behind your right shoulder. Then you surprise yourself by placing Beth behind your left. You turn your head and smile at one neighbour in the circle. Then you turn it the other way and smile at the other one.

The meeting begins. People talk. You listen as best you can. Your turn comes.

"Hi," you say, and you feel tears burbling up as you say it, ugly tears. "My name is Kaya and I'm a heroin addict. I want to tell you . . ." And you do. You tell. You say the big bits, one after the other. It only takes a minute. Less, really. You stop. Someone places a box of tissues in your lap, and you cry through the whole rest of the meeting, quietly, since other people are telling their stories now.

At the end of the meeting you collect yourself, put the tissue box with the others on the side table and say goodbye to three people on the way out. You discover real empathy in their eyes. You hope they can see it in yours.

Δ

"We're going swimming," Beth says on Saturday. You don't argue.

And when you step inside the doors at the pool and smell the chlorine, you have to fight the tears that try to get out of you. It's been a long time since you smelled that smell. You don't wait for Beth; you don't bother locking up your stuff or digging your towel out of your bag. You just head on through, winding an elastic around your hair. A ten-second shower, a shallow dive off the side of the pool, and you're in.

You head for the bottom, and turn and look up when you get there, eyes wide, taking it all in. You see legs, bodies, and the shifty enclosed space above the water. No moon here. Still, it's fabulous!

You have no idea how long you spend like that, coming

up now and again for a breath, but when you return to the side at last, you stop and stare. Those girls are following you everywhere! They are all there in a row, sitting on the side of the pool, feet in the water.

"We thought they'd have to come and drag you out with a net," Marlene says.

"The lifeguard says no diving off the side," Beth adds.

Samantha and Michelle are talking to each other, paying no attention. Diana looks a bit tentative, but she slides into the water, grimacing as it passes her waist and then her chest.

"I'm going to go swim properly," Jane says as she hoists herself to her feet and heads for the lanes.

You swim up to Diana and poke her in the arm. "Come under with me," you say.

And she looks at you, treading water hard as she considers. Is that a tiny smile on her face? You look into her eyes. Yes!

She squeezes those eyes shut, then tips forward and kicks herself down deep. You follow.

Δ

Swimming is the best part of those first weeks. And painting. You paint a lot, big paintings, ugly ones. Painting, you are determined, is going to belong to you, not to that man.

Therapy's the worst. Or the hardest. In therapy there's nowhere to hide. You sit, the two of you, on your straight-backed chairs, knees facing. And she directs. And redirects. You watch her face for cues, for horror, for pity, but she is solid as a brick.

She does not ask the question that has screamed itself forever in your head, the question you long to drown out any way you can. They have been stripping the means away from you: the drugs, the endless stream of men with their collection of needs and desires, some of them twisted, a few dangerous, most of them duller than dirty snow.

Why did you keep going back?

To be more precise, it is not the question that screams at you: it's the answers. The answers that turn every atom of you into filth.

He didn't make you, did he?

It must be all your fault.

You must have wanted it.

You must have liked it.

It felt good when he touched you, didn't it?

The therapist does not ask. She just looks. She just sits there like a big person-shaped brick. Directing and redirecting. Asking about everything else, every single little thing. Until, at last, you break.

"That's what you want me to say, isn't it," you scream, on your feet now. "It felt good. Yeah, sure. It felt good. It felt bad. It felt disgusting. It hurt." And you stand, like an animal, on the far side of the room from the therapist, who sits and looks at you calmly, as if the world has not just collapsed on you both.

Not like a brick, more like a great big sponge, the therapist sits and looks at you and soaks up the horror of it, soaks it up without getting tainted by it. No, a sponge isn't right either.

"He had to make you like it," she says, once your breathing has slowed, once you are edging back toward your chair, "or you would never have gone back."

You sink back onto your chair and stare at her. The truth of what she has just said, so obvious. *He had to make you like it, or you would never have gone back.* In that moment, the two parts join and become one. The tea, the toys, the roses, the stories. And what happened down in that basement room.

With that comes a glimmer. Mr. G was not kind. He was never, not for one single moment, kind.

EPILOGUE

Me (Kaya)

It's strange looking back on all that now.

It's not as if life got so perfect then. I still had all of it to deal with.

I even relapsed once, a month or two in. I took off downtown for a few days and used again and worked to pay for it. Everything. Mom called Raven and Raven found me, got me back in treatment. I'll never forget that moment when she came up to me on the street. I was leaning against a wall, just gearing up to get money for my next fix, and there she was. Not one bit of judgment in her eyes. Just love, really. And understanding. All the toughness ran off me, just melted away, and I went. And in treatment that time, I talked.

Therapy was a bit different after that. Something had opened up inside me, even though it was still easier for me to write about stuff happening to "you" not "me." She's still trying to get me to write that *I* was sad, that *I* felt horror, but so far, it hasn't worked. I can write the words, but they don't mean anything. They don't connect. So she lets me keep on writing *you.*

Diana started seeing her too. Diana and I don't see each other much now, but we don't have to hide from each other either. She and Michelle have connected, which is great for both of them, I guess, since Michelle and I don't have a whole lot to say to each other anymore either. Marlene, though, has become a friend, though her mom and dad seem nervous around me.

And we, Marlene and I, I mean, have been coming up with a plan. I told her I thought her grandfather must have had other victims. I told her about all the drawings. We want to get our hands on them and see if we can find anybody else. There are a lot of obstacles . . . A lot. But at least we're talking about it. There's got to be something we can do, some way we can help those other girls.

We could start by talking to her mom and dad. She told me that she sat them down one day and got them talking, brought it all out in the open, the bath, what her mom thought about it, why her mom wouldn't let her see her grandfather anymore.

"They don't want to think about the other kids, though," Marlene said, looking me in the eye, "but maybe if they thought of helping them instead of just feeling guilty . . ." She paused, still staring at me, so I finished for her.

"Maybe if they heard from me too."

I could tell she knew that was tough for me to say. I'm not exactly keen on talking to Mr. G's son about what happened to me. His granddaughter, I can totally handle—at least, I can now—but his son . . . I'll do it, though, because now I know that talking and helping are two ways you make things better, even if the talking part hurts.

Δ

Like I said, almost a year has gone by now. I've been clean since that one time, though often I'm really white-knuckling it. I keep right on wanting to go back downtown. And I know that's not good. I've stuck it out at home, though. I'm even going to school, most mornings.

In the afternoons, I stay home and I write. My own private version of home schooling, I guess. I hand my pages over to my therapist every couple of weeks, and she reads them and talks with me about them. It's this story, of course. I've worked like a dog on it. I'm lucky I had that prison notebook tucked away. It made tough reading, but it gave me a start.

I didn't write Beth's parts, of course. She wrote them herself. She wrote sections and gave them to me. It kind of changed things for me to see how it all was from her point of view. We're getting closer now, which is a big surprise and pretty great.

But she hasn't read my parts yet. I'm going to give her the whole thing to read as soon as I'm done. I still have two more things to write about. Then I'll print it out for her.

I'm working on something else for her too. Her birthday's not till October, but I missed her last one, and I didn't really have anything for her for Christmas either. I went and asked Mr. Holbrook if I could sign up for Metalwork 101 again and told him about my idea. I'm making her a mobile with some of that glass of hers (which I had to take without telling her). Making it balance is tricky, but when it does, and the glass, with thin wire circle holding it in place, sways when you touch it, it's pretty satisfying. If she can hang it in the sun . . .

Right after her birthday, I'm going into a residential treatment program. Two weeks. I'm hoping that'll help. It would be so easy to use again. Just once. That's what I say to myself when I wake up in the night, shaking: I could feel that perfect escape just one more time and then quit for good after that. I remind myself about detox, how awful it was—both times—but a lot of the time, the memory of the release is a lot stronger than the memory of the pain. So, yeah, two weeks of treatment . . .

Δ

This morning, Beth and Mom and I went to the memorial for the missing women. I really went for Sarah, since I didn't know any of the others. Beth and Mom went to be there for me. We snuck past all those TV cameras, but at the entrance, three women were burning sweetgrass in a great big shell and smudging everyone, sweeping a feather up and down near our bodies. I washed myself from head to toe with that smoke. I'll bet I had ancestors who did that too. It was crazy. While I was doing it I cried and cried, and the woman with the feather just smiled a small smile. I felt something like a hairline crack forming right through my heart, and that smoke slipped in through that crack and flushed some of the black guck out of there.

I'll have to tell my therapist about that.

At last I was finished, and I put my rings back on while Mom and Beth took their turns. They were a lot quicker than

I was. Inside, we went up to the balcony. I thought we might be away from the crowd up there, but we weren't. The whole place was jammed. Right to the rafters, Mom said.

Then, behind me, "Hey, Kaya." It was Raven.

I looked at her and started to cry again, but this was different, not a hairline crack letting in healing smoke, but a grief too big, way, way too big, for anything. Raven climbed right over into my pew, and we cried together, the two of us. Once again, Mom and Beth waited patiently. Then the event began. Some of it was kind of religious and just washed over me, but there was a time when anyone could get up and speak. The line snaked across the stage and down the central aisle. I listened and listened; every bit of me listened. And remembered. I looked over and saw tears on Beth's and Mom's faces. Not on Raven's, though. She'd cried herself out, maybe.

After a bit, Raven went down and joined the line. For a moment I thought about following her. I didn't, though. I was there to say a quiet goodbye, not just to Sarah, but to that whole terrible part of my life. I didn't need a podium to do that.

I brought my hands together in my lap, fingertips touching. "Goodbye," I whispered.

Δ

The park—one near our house, not downtown— was dark, lit only by the streetlights on Trimble Street. The grass was damp, the ground soft. I took off at a run, and when I reached the enormous swing-set I turned back. Beth was standing at the edge of the grass, probably unnerved by the dark and the clanking and whooshing of a kid practising on his skateboard at midnight.

"Come on!" I shouted, and she did—not running, though.

I grinned, kicked off my shoes and plunked myself onto a swing. Pumping my legs furiously, I reached for the sky with my toes.

Beth kept her shoes on. She shoved her small pink rabbit into her pocket, grabbed the chains on the swing beside mine and leaned back onto the seat. I swept past her, legs stretched out in front, hair flying. Beth had to work hard to catch up.

For long minutes we swung together, caught up in the motion, competing for the sky. The metal frame lurched. "Whoa," we cried as our stomachs tried to push up our throats. Together, we slowed down.

For a while we drifted back and forth, feet held off the sand.

I could feel Beth struggling to speak. Finally, she pushed out the words. "Are you . . . going to stay home now, Kaya?"

I kept my eyes on the ground. "You're my sister, not my mother," I said. My voice was calm. Then I looked at Beth and smiled.

Beth pushed off sideways with a foot and snuck a hand into her pocket. With a grand flourish, she whisked that pink rabbit out of my hood. "But I can work miracles," she said.

I grabbed the rabbit and laughed. "Save that for the stage," I said.

"Sure," Beth said. "As long as you'll be there to watch."

"You know I will," I said.

AFTERWORD

My sister, Sarah de Vries, is one of the missing women from Vancouver's Downtown Eastside. I have written about her and shared some of her writing in another book, *Missing Sarah: A Memoir of Loss*, which was published in 2003 and came out in a new edition in 2008. Not long after that, a woman came to me to tell me that a man in our neighbourhood sexually abused my sister for a number of years when Sarah was a little girl. I believed this woman because what she told me helped me make sense of so many things in Sarah's life, and because she had reason to know.

It was shocking news, horrible to learn that Sarah had suffered in that way when she was a little girl, and that she never told us, to realize that her suffering began so much earlier than we knew. I found myself haunted by this new information, trying to take it in, to understand this new part of my sister's experience, and her silence. *Rabbit Ears* arose from that haunting.

The story is fiction. Kaya is based on Sarah in many ways, but Kaya's family is not Sarah's, and Kaya's experiences are drawn largely from my imagination. I struggled when I faced writing about her time downtown, until I realized that she could meet Sarah there. That's what caused me to set the story back a little bit in time, to when Sarah was still alive. It was a joy, for me, writing Sarah to life. The scene on the swings in CRAB Park is drawn from a story a woman told me about her and Sarah. I changed its location. The memorial stone in CRAB Park is real, and was put in place in 1997. The corner, Princess and Hastings, is where my sister worked, and it is from that corner that she disappeared on April 14, 1998. The little grey house is also real. And I remember spilled pudding. And a scrawny kitten. And that glorious garden.

The story was always called *Rabbit Ears*. I liked the title. When I was working on revisions, I spoke to a Women's Studies class and showed them an interview Sarah gave the CBC back in 1993. In the interview, she talks about being a heroin addict and advises viewers to stay away from the drug. She is eloquent, and I'm proud of her for giving that interview. I show it often.

This time, though, about halfway through, I noticed what looked like the tips of two ears on Sarah's chest. I stared, hoping, hoping the camera would dip lower. At the end, I queried the class. Had I seen what I thought I had seen? I had. My sister had a Playboy Bunny tattooed on the top of her left breast. I had seen it before. Of course I had. But I had never thought about what the image was. My book is called *Rabbit Ears* because the older sister loves magic. I had no idea that it also draws its title from my sister's tattoo. I came out of that Women's Studies class feeling that Sarah had given me her blessing.

I wanted to tell a story about a girl who went through what my sister went through, but survived, a story about a girl who broke the silence that was holding her prisoner, a story about a group of girls who paid attention, who reached out. I believe in these possibilities for Kaya and for each one of us.

ACKNOWLEDGEMENTS

I thank Sarah's childhood friend for coming to me, for telling me about the abuse. I know how much courage that took, and I am forever grateful.

I thank Christianne Hayward and the teens and mothers at Christianne's Lyceum for reading my manuscript and sharing your feedback. It was enormously helpful. Thank you also, Roberta.

I thank everyone who worked on the manuscript. Hadley Dyer, my editor at HarperCollins: you were thorough, thoughtful, kind and patient—everything a person hopes for in an editor and much that a person doesn't dare dream of. Freelance editors Catharine Chen and Sophie Tupholme: you read the manuscript at a critical time and helped me to feel that I was on the right track. Allyson Latta, my copyeditor: I so appreciate your attention to detail and your personal touch. Production editor Maria Golikova, thank you for shepherding Beth and Kaya's story so graciously. And Kelly

Jones, proofreader, thank you for taking such care with that crucial last step.

I thank writing buddies Rachel Rose and Lori Shenher, and my friend Kerry Porth: your kind words helped me carry on and your suggestions made the book better. And I thank Raven for enthusiastically allowing me to use her name in this story.

I gratefully acknowledge the Canada Council for the Arts for the grant that assissted in the writing of this book.

And I thank my husband, Roland, the first to read all my stories.